DRAGON
DAYS

DRAGON DAYS

TODD FRENCH

ReadersMagnet, LLC

TABLE OF CONTENTS

1 John 2:17
English Standard Version
[17]"And the world is passing away along with its desires,
but whoever does the will of God abides forever."

"Life is made up of marble and mud."
—**Nathaniel Hawthorne**

VANGUARD FIRE DANCE TROOP/PARK WALK 03/27/22

There are moments-just moments-when we 'round a corner or path
And come across the quick fleet feet-beat of beauty and wonder's leavings
That's what I felt when I circled the green hollow of the park's bowl
And there under the late afternoon's eucalyptus and cedar shade
I saw the banners and drums laid out and the young Asian people
Garbed in black and red taking team photos after wrapping flag practice
Others in red and gold standing sentry near the scarlet drums
Headbands trailing in the breeze percussion sticks in hand
The head of a lion-dragon costume lying in the grass bright as dreams
You couldn't help but be moved by the tableau of team brio and cheerful closure
The infectious joy and laughter of a good work-out and cultural share
Led me down the path like the fragrant rodeo loop from a celebratory meal
I felt a pang because it was done-the pounding skins and swooping flags
But I was happy for them because they were happy
Like walking by a church when the bride and groom are rushing by pelted with
rice
I smiled at the clowning and good-natured cut ups as they posed
(of course some girls in the front rank dangled their buddy upside down)
And my eyes went to the rippling black banner with red tails speaking wind-
speak
Like a plane of gust-strafed lake water on a cloudy, starless night
A school of red carp hitting the bugs at the bank's muddy verge
Or the last few flints of a dead campfire's fume swept upwards
Into the moonless dark while someone eases a guitar strap
And someone else says let's get the empties in the morning

Or drops of blood flying from a warlord's black lacquered breastplate

As he hugs the neck of his dark charger screaming we'll regroup later

And come around behind south of the marshes with the reeds for a screen

Or a thief dropping a handful of rubies as he passed the sleeper's bed

The others banners-gold and red blazed and danced like flames

Twisting sinuously around wall after wall of summer oak and dogwood

And I had just missed it

I could see it all through the imagination's eye

The water-ravel and undulance of cloth, the unfettered flight of silk and sunlight

The sole's refute of grass and gravity, perfect interweave of bodies and balance

The timing of skins' thunder the toll and roll of drum-fire slow/rapid/louder/
faster

Swift slide/muscle/bone/tendon stretch/silk scissor of viridescence and tree
shadow

Balance of flag-pole/up-thrust to blue and cumulus scud

Celebration of country and color's conflagration

Ground pounded by grace and skill

Swept over by sound's stour

Storm beat after beat fire form and flag leap lightning youth's arete

Braise of banner banked by greensward birds banking startled by drum thrum

I could imagine it all as I watched the troop bag up their costumes and props

And made ready to leave (one of them told me they would be back next year)

I could imagine it all as I made my second pass around the bowl later in the day

Flag foot arm hand poise percussion cannonade of time body space held sway

Now reduced to trammeled grass threaded here and there with sunset's embers

The breeze a bit colder

The shadow a little longer

I took it in with sad regret

Missing out on one of spring's first revels

And I hoped I would catch it next year

EXECUTIVE ORDERS

Not that you would ever hold an obsidian knife
To free the "glorious pomegranate" from its bone-cage
And hold it aloft in the brash blood-orange wash of an Aztec dawn
Standing at the pyramid apex to honor Tlaloc the rain god
(Aztecs would have supported your Climate Change riffs Joe)
Or Huitzilopochtli or Chalchitilcue some pop-eyed and fang-hung stone
Hungry as puma or jaguarundi for hearts and choice cuts
No you would never hold the dagger plunge it in and salute the sun
Surrounded by gilded skull-racks and feathers from quetzal or macaw
But as a priest of The Woke you're doing a solid job
I thought someone should tell you that Mr. President
Our freedoms and liberties falling under the scribble of your pen
What is it 42 or 44 executive orders I forget
Lives and livelihoods piling up a like a line-up of atrocities
On a Mesoamerican sacrifice calendar
Do you even look at what you are signing Joe
Can you hear the cries of the unborn to fall under your signature
The wails of the eunuchs you will make of our youths
The suicide screams of our daughters on hormone-blockers
Where is your soul hiding like a fever-shivered monkey
In a green hell of screaming birds and jaguar calls
Clinging to a ziggurat's gore-slicked side like a gecko
Hanging on incoherent taking orders from who was it again?

ROYAL PALMS

Who cleaned up, swept up, sacked up the palm leaves when the King went out?
Who bagged them up in despair or reverence looking over their shoulders,
Making sure a quick-eyed Pharisee or centurion didn't misinterpret the tears
Be they grief-grief for the dogwood cross and hill-or angry disappointment,
The clenching of a hand, gnawing of a lower lip as the streets were swept
Of royalty's sigils of ragged, pleated green long trampled to shreds and tatters,
Removed with embarrassment by some because Maccabees mail and buckler,
Didn't descend on the carpenter-king-Roman
eagles shattered and turned to molten gold,
Piles of red scutum shields with thunder bolts and legion numbers heaped,
Like weathered tile slates, burned to the quick by angel-fire's sweeping beam,
(No, the children of Israel wouldn't burn them for seven years eschewing
firewood)
Barracks fuming like an old bore's pipe in the Judean sunset's purple and red,
What was expected-crown sword insurrection freedom fragrant as rosemary,
(there was freedom yes there was but it was not what they expected)
(it was not the freedom-carmine-handed and hate-throated-for which they
elected)
David's Heir didn't call for war and massacre against the empire of Augustus,
This rain-dribble of cuirasses and heat-beaten helms holding the Levant,
How many-blind to the grace in the blood that
was shed-knelt and scooped up the fronds
The fronds fanned the Man and the sweaty, fly-stung colt (horse dumb to
epiphany),
Tore them into bits while the priests, phylacteries nodding from head and arm,
Signaled their sour approval, faces strained and opaque to pity and remorse,

But warmed and reassured that mobs were fickle, quick to love and hate;

But they would get another chance when old Bar Kokbha got their hopes up,

Son of a (dead, collapsing) Star-Deception's guttering

candle nub-blind light blind guide,

But here at least the priests, scribes and lawyers were agreed:

It was over-over and done-the end-come to nothing but the end.

But I wonder if a young Roman legionnaire, dry and thin as the Daucus Carota,

Hair prematurely white as the Palestine iris or canary clover,

Eyes brown as the hills of Moab-pale circles on his neck where the cord

That had secured the little Mithras bull charm had been snapped,

Its light burden flung into the midden heap

behind the barracks or a lentil pot shop,

I wonder if that young soldier,

who had seen Mary's son stumbling up to the skull hill,

Weighed down with the cross, with the spit and insults of the mob,

The lash rising and falling, sending the grasshoppers and flies flying,

settling, flying again,

I wonder if afterwards, after it was done, that perhaps on his way back to the

camp,

He found some of last Sunday's palms scattered here and there,

Unaccounted for, half-buried under the long day's dust, dirt and skat,

Stamped into the ground by the passing weight of man,

horse, donkey, sheep and goat,

And he remembered how the people who mocked and cursed,

Zhrusting forth reviling fists,

Had waved them-had laid them down Sunday

last before the humble man on the young colt,

And if he had heard those words at the end,

"Father, forgive them, they know not what they do."

Maybe the young soldier shuffled back, armored cuirass clanging and abrading,

A dryness in his mouth the water,

vinegar and coriander of his canteen sponge couldn't assuage,

(he'd seen The Man refuse the same when they lifted up

the same posca on the spear to him)

(they had verbally abused the teacher but acknowledged the dying flesh)

And he found himself-mind aswirl in what he had

seen-unconsciously picking at the cord,
That held the Bull against his throat-picking at it,
turning the knot until he tugged it off,
(in a land where messiahs and insurrectionists sprang up
like rabbits you needed god, yes?)
(the Bull was a good fit-no women allowed-and you
passed the ranks as Crow, Soldier, Lion)
(Courtier of The Sun and then Father-good enough
for those who lived by pilum and sword)
The wonder of what he'd seen on Golgotha reducing the city's din in his ears to
The corkscrew of sea-sibilance as in the pink/blue whorls of a shell,
The crying of the women, the arguments of the priests and scribes,
Nothing more than low bee-fuzz on the salt-stained auricle and lobes.
Maybe, looking right and left, one hand holding the armor's plates close as he
bent,
He tore off a pleated section of palm, stamped flat, crushed by a thousand sandals,
Praying that some drinking buddy didn't hoof it over red-faced and puffing,
Hissing/or shouting what are you doing Lucius what are you doing, doing there?
Thinking about the lacerated and beaten figure hoisted upward,
Drops of blood dark as pomegranate seeds on the crown of thorns,
The forgiveness in the words-the day's early dark/earth
clearing its stone-filled throat,
Shaking under his feet their feet dumping the spear-wielder on his ass,
The flowing fringe-winged shadows of carrion birds already claiming the thieves,
Those words ("It is finished"),
already working at undoing the cord that held the Bull,
(the ranks of Crow, Soldier, Lion, Sun Courtier and Father undoing themselves)
(undoing themselves unspeaking themselves in his heart whispering in his ears)
The words, long fingers scrabbling at the chipped and worn soap-stone beast,
All the old understandings and reasoning adrift
as fishermen's boats on blue-greens sea,
The sand particles under his sandals screaming some secret, expansive grief,
All of it working at his soul as if he were taxed by something (something)
That worked through thoughts and emotions executing some relentless
decimation,
Every tenth truth struck down with the sword's edge of those simple words,

("Father, forgive them, they know not what they do")

The silver ripple/rise and fall/of the spirit's gladius/pugio/pilum

cutting everything down,

Like a Zealot's blade flashing from the crowd unseaming

the guts of a lax Herodian guard,

(How how how could someone forgive those who did that? Who could forgive?)

(How how could someone love the crucifiers/scourgers/

spitters and take such pain and love?)

(How do you forgive the soldiers who swigged sour wine and laughed?)

(how do you forgive the priests swaddled in their robes,

phylacteries ruffled and bobbing)

And did he see something past The Man's final words,

spirit wafted away like thistle,

Did his inward eye spied a world's brimming cup of over-awing legion standards,

Eagle, boar, wolf, horse, minotaur, serpent *Imago* covered by white doves,

Weighed down like the sails of triremes and biremes by terns and gulls,

Could he just stumble back to dice with the Syrian brothers or the African

Marcian,

Discuss the merits of the new girl at Alexander's place (fresh from Parthia),

How could you talk about *that kind of love* in the face of what you just saw,

How did the heart not flood like the Tiber with the enormity of the love?

Maybe as he straightened, placing the King's fan between tunic and skin,

He surprised the gaze of a young girl across the square in dust-spackled robes,

Squirreling away a dusty fragment of her own,

her tresses peeking from her head covering,

Like bunches of black grapes,

her hazel eyes going wide then lighting with recognition,

When she saw that he was doing the same in that lull of foot traffic,

Her mouth quirking into the start of-hope/ironic mirth/gratitude to see another?

(Another what? What did it all mean-what was starting with this simple gesture)

(what were they both buying into it-could it even be put down in words)

And maybe the legionnaire with a look as questioning as her own,

Hands shaking, not sure why but unable

to forget the human standard raised to the sky,

Some power unknown unnamed indescribable

that stood as the Aquilifer on the skull-hill,

Raising a banner of bone flesh sinew spirit more more
that would outlast eagle and imago,
That would outlast home host posting barracks pilum gladius pugio road file
testudo
Bridge wages cuirass sandal laurel myrtle olive wreath battle brain pushing it all
Grappling with that, seeing the girl whisk away the frond's finger,
face softening in cloth folds,
Seeing the Man's pain, the blood-stars of hand forced open by the hard nails,
Maybe unspeaking he sent a surfeit of unresolved thoughts across the street to
her,
Seeking understanding in her perplexity as much as giving it,
As they pocketed these small remains of the triumphal entry,
I don't know
I don't know
But it could be
It could be
It could be
Something could be

THE RUSSIANS IN CHERNOBYL

I stand in awe of you, Apollyon's argonauts-honestly, I do:
My hackles rise, my tongue cleaves to the roof of my mouth
as I consider your works,
Soldier, soldier, burning bright in the irradiated forests of the night,
How your commanders have hammered out and formed your fearful symmetry!
Before I saw the satellite photos of the mass graves of the 9000 victims,
Which you left in the battered Ukrainian city of Mariupol,
I read how you captured the nuclear power plant of Chernobyl,
Fearless, heedless, heartless Morlocks, exercising troglodyte civilities and
valiancies,
Limbic brain alight with the promises of these dragon days of fire,
blood and adamantine scale,
I read how you motored your way into the radioactive Red Forest in your armor,
(the trees are red due to aftermath of the plant's 1986 reactor disaster)
No Hazmat/radiation gear for you
(they wouldn't have helped as bad as the contamination is),
But in you went and set to: rolled in with your tanks and started digging trenches,
(when the going gets dark, the dark of heart get going)
Kicking up the death dust-spreading more death and sickness,
Endangering other countries from the clouds you raised and dispersed,
(what did you care-it was the easiest access route to Kyiv)
Taking/breathing/sweating extinction bit by bit even as you advanced,
The angel of the Lord breathing on Sennacherib in slow time,
Until the conditions to which you were exposed drove you out of Chernobyl.
And now hundreds of you are being treated in Belarus,
For acute radiation sickness and also frostbite (they gave you no cold garb).

Those who called you to war do not care about your lives and loves,

And the man drenched in gore who stood up at midnight Orthodox Easter Mass,

Who said, "Truly, He is risen," will not raise you up from your sickbed.

I have seen the things you have done in Bucha and Mariupol,

As if we have gone back to the savage, ancient days when

The Bulgarian Khan Krum and the Byzantine Emperor Leo

Traded atrocity for atrocity-children's heads smashed against rocks,

Royal skulls lined with gold and turned into drinking mugs.

What you have brought to the game feels like those days of Krum and Leo,

That sinecures of darkness are being filled everywhere by guardian demons

And devils everywhere are rejoicing over these dragon days.

Even so, I can find it in my heart to pray:

That you repudiate blood and find your way to the Lamb.

That that you repudiate blood and find your way to the Lamb.

For the sake of your souls, may you repudiate blood and find your way

To the Lamb.

ILHAN LOVES TO FLY

I am not sure why the Muslim congresswoman (formerly of Somalia)
Was so beside herself with Twitter-fed indignation that she had to post
An angry/sarcastic tant about the Christian singer plying his guitar on her flight,
After all, I am sure that if you had boarded a flight from Riyadh,
Or maybe Dubai, the prayers would be coming over the loudspeakers,
Frankly, I really don't think it's a bad time to beseech the Almighty
(Whomever/Whatever you wish to address your prayers to)
 When you are swung heavenward in a metal tube through
Ragged Merino sheep coat of cloud into sun-shot cerulean blue,
Over the scintillant net of the wide and endless Pacific,
Nothing between you and oblivion but long cabin and human skill.
What if she had gotten up to share a prayer of her own faith,
Or to sing a song of her homeland-would folks have listened with a good will?
(she wondered in a huff what would have happened if she had started praying)
Oh, I think so: if I had been there, I suspect I would have recorded the moment,
Or looked up the story after decompressing in my hotel room.
But come on, now…
When the passenger jet starts *thump-thumping* down the runway,
With the unsteady lurch of a half-chewed stegosaurus,
Making a last valiant suicide run and tail-swipe at a Tyrannosaurus Rex,
When those gas turbine engines roar into life-don't we all become believers,
Those that already were doubly so, and those that never were,
Suddenly entreating God (some God) some angel some devil
But not old Gaia whose gift of gravity you have slipped with such ease?
The flint-eyed atheist, the dreamy agnostic, the most committed Satanist
(though what help they would expect from *him* is beyond me),

The most righteous pastor and the richest billionaire,

The selfie-sipping Instagram model with her millions of hits,

The most war-tested veteran, the newlyweds, the grandparents

Off to Hawaii to celebrate their 50th Wedding Anniversary,

Everyone's heart skips-like the hiker who unplugs from their buds,

And turns to find a bear happily shambling after them on the wood path,

All of us, in that crippled cadence of wheel-bump turning to *rise rise rise,*

As the amenities of free agency and ambulatory elan are whited out/blotted out,

And all bets-our future, our loves, hopes, ambitions-are scattered like chaff,

Until grace descends (for some) with the flight attendant's mellifluous tones,

And the prayers, entreaties, promises, vows are subsumed in relief,

Fears and anxieties tamped down like the last

smoking fire-pit coals under a boot-heel.

And God-talk gives way (for some) to in-flight movies,

phone texts, books, journals, Twitter…

Fears of lighting/malfunctions/collisions/terrorists/psychopaths

are rubbish-binned by most.

Except for turbulence when God-talk pops up like a

martin's head from a pile of snow,

Then ducks its head down.

But others continue the dialogue through the dazzling day or star-glimmered

night.

Doesn't the congresswoman from Minnesota realize that we all deal as best we

can,

With the helplessness we feel in the narrow nave of The Church of The Airborne,

That faith in metal/fuel/fallible human skill and training makes us all believers,

Downing our wafers and wine in the certainty of a safe landing,

Followed by the joy of hands scrabbling for suitcases,

bodies pouring into the passage,

The shared communion dissipating with the reaffirmation

of gravity/earth-anchored flesh,

The objects of our love, or the promise of new/old attachments, journeys/quests,

Beyond the baggage carousel,

the taxi/rented car wend into brindled noon or storm-lashed dark,

The sermon ended, the lesson ended-life resumed,

safety presumed, until the return home.

Doesn't the flyer from Minnesota understand that the Christian preacher
Up-jumped from his seat and strumming the chords on his instrument,
Is simply providing the act of removing fear and unease from the pressurized air,
As a good broom removes the cobwebs from the corners of an old room.
It could have been some comedian getting up to give us an impression of
President Biden or President Trump-or a child singing Panis Angelicus,
Or a retiree with a Great Fish Story from Vilnius in Lithuania,
Or a refugee from the war-torn Ukraine telling us how much she appreciates
The new opportunities afforded her where she is heading.
We all deal with the marriage of fear/cerulean blue/land's loss/steel and fire
As best we can.

A DOG ON A VESPA

When the late afternoon's arterial hues shades into twilight's magenta bruise,
What would we not give-frustrated, weary, disconsolate,
The giving heart gone hard and ferried down
sluggish canals by grumbling gondoliers,
If all of it was just upended, blown away by a stray in joyous sputter and put-put?
What if, as the sprinkler timers went off, and dinner was just underway,
If a red cocker-spaniel blasted down the block on a red and gold Vespa,
Barking deliriously, happy beyond reason, shaggy ears trailing like windsocks,
Lips fluttering back from a wide doggy grin like a cuttlefish rumba,
Tongue pulled sidewise by the breeze like a fashionable ascot
Wound around the neck of a racing-ace at the 24 Hours of Le Mans,
Brown, intelligent eyes laughing, sparkling behind tinted aviator's goggles,
While one reddish-brown paw taps-taps the air-horn.
What wouldn't you give to be dropped to the grass in gut-busting hilarity,
To be doubled over in a paroxysm of emphysematous surrender,
If you could end each day-no matter the weight, the freight, the heartbreak,
With a bowwow with brio and horsepower flying back and forth before your
lawn,
Cats and squirrels taking to the trees, confetti-webs and accordion pleats
Of shredded bark sailing down in their wake?
Who'd fill the air with a veritable northeaster of bacon and dog biscuit,
A proper edible ticker tape treat, for a goodwill hero keeping his seat?
Who'd stand there, lobbing Milk Bones and chips of jerky like carob pods,
A direct hit to the teeth and gums with every try-and the reward for us,
A death-defying doggie handstand on the handlebars, hind feet rowing the air.
There are times in the midst of these dragon days of internal weariness and braise,

I would give anything to see a cocker-spaniel on a Vespa fly by at dusk,
To see the kids and their dogs at the curb making their noise,
Waving, barking, cheering, chuffing: smiles breaking out like a virus chain
Across every uptilted face, whiskery muzzle,
Young couples and old with their arms around each other's waists,
Toddlers perched on top of their parents' shoulders or cradled in their arms,
Hummingbirds going up and up in in water-spout spirals, flashing, fanning,
Flying side to side in cartoon arrow caricatures, interweaving in feathery arabesques,
Even bats would belly up to the challenge in their leathery fusillades,
Their missiles making black blots of mean mortician ties,
Every finch and sparrow trill their lungs out, cheep-cheeping in atavistic exultation,
Even the crows in the cedars would be stunned to silence at such japery and jounce.
I would love to see the whole block turned out until purple/violet light fades,
And God straightens out the moon's crumpled up boneyard sketch,
The stars making their faintest pin-pricks in the magic hour's fading scrim of sky.
What a show if we could for a while forget our cares that way,
The heart punched up like a pillow-every swell candescent cell,
Sawing away like Lindsey Sterling on her violin or Tina Guo on her cello,
While a bowwow with brio, horsepower and style flies by,
Doing his best to provide a proper send-off for the pains of the day.

PRESIDENT VLADIMIR PUTIN AT EASTER MASS

The irony was not lost to me: that you had filled so many tombs this spring,

And here you were celebrating the day that The Lord rose from His tomb,

After offering Himself as the substitutionary sacrifice for the sins of the world.

There was something distinctly medieval

about the audacity and unabashed evil of it,

The barbaric hypocrisy of scratching the ears of feral, half-starved hounds

Before kicking them into a bear-pit or holding cockfights

in the cellar of a bishop's house,

Something dim and baleful as light's refraction

from unfaceted gems on cold iron crowns.

(what Jesus did you pray to what Jesus did your pray to what Jesus heard you)

Here you were, observing the most candescent of truths while your soldiers

Performed the miracles of de-animation of limb, hope and dreams in the Ukraine.

I reflected on an infinitely finer Vladimir who brought his people to Christ,

Who dragged his people out of the starless mud fields of paganism,

Tossing Perun The Striker, god of thunder,

with his silver moustaches into the river Dnieper,

Taking the sister, Anna, of the East Roman Basileus Basil for his wife,

(six thousand Varangians went to the Bulgar-slayer

as a fair trade for a Byzantine bride).

Now, you, Vladimir of the Russians battled the Volodymyr of the Ukraine,

This weekend when the Orthodox world celebrated

the victory of the Lamb of The World,

One of you striving for mastery, the other for his people's naked lives,

What were you thinking as you took your place in the sanctuary?

What informed your feelings: exaltation, guilt, shame, hauteur?
Did the voices of the Ukrainian dead whisper like birch trees in a winter breeze:
"How could you dare to take communion, how could you dare to share in it?"
And as I watched this play out before the altar, I, an American who loves your land,
Your literature, your music, your artists and culture, I couldn't help see parallels:
Like Tsar Ivan the Terrible sending lists of his victims to the Russian monasteries
So the monks might pray for the souls of those
his broom and wolf's head lugging Oprichniks
Had hunted down upon his orders when he divided
his realm after his fake abdication.
And to be sure you looked ill at ease and fidgety with your red candle,
Even as Patriarch Kirill and the other Orthodox churchmen
who approved your unprovoked war,
Clad in their scintillant white robes and tiaras, swinging their incense censers,
Intoning the holy words of the midnight mass with piety,
observing the proper rites,
"Truly He is Risen," you responded, and yet to my eye, you looked ill,
Perhaps embarrassed that you could say those words ("Truly He is Risen")
On those defending life, limb, love and family in Mariupol,
Odesa, Kharkiv, Ocheretyne,
There would still be some exchange of the painted Pysanka eggs,
The beautifully decorated Easter bread, Paska made with three loaves,
(To honor nature, to honor the dead and to honor the living),
The ringing bells-somehow-in the Ukraine and in Russia-people would find a way,
To remember the Son who died on the dogwood cross,
Whether they knelt in the glass and rubble of their home, or gutted churches,
They would find a way to paint the Pysanka eggs red as the strawberry owls,
Or the turquoise and gold of breaking dawn-they would find the colors somehow.
"Truly He is Risen," would go from lips to lips-mouths shaking with war's palsy.
The open tomb and victory would be remembered, in spite of the loss and horror.
Did the voices of the parents of dead Russian soldiers moan like wind through
broken window panes and rifts of twisted steel and stone in the sides of office
buildings "How could you dare to take communion-you who have the blood of
our children on your hands?" How could you believe

His blood has washed away your sins?"
As you stood there with your red candle
at Christ The Saviour Cathedral in Moscow,
Enjoying the sensual pull of liturgical chants, the gold dome, the arched ceilings,
Mosaics, transcendent beauty of icons/iconotasis
of apostles, saint, saviour and mother,
The overpowering meet of light and faith like the crossed contrails of falling stars,
The holy smell of beeswax and incense roiling in perfumed clouds.
Did you see the three-headed shadow of the dragon Zmey Gorynych
Bobbing and fanning its wings on the far walls and did he hiss,
"You did nothing wrong-unlike Bogatyr Dobrynya Nikitich-you did not
Ride into the Saracen Mountains, and you did not trample baby dragons,
So, I for one will grant you absolution-I will remit it all,
And for any you may wage in Moldova and Georgia, for these are dragon days,
And you are a Tsar Vladimir that I can see eye to eye with, unlike the one
Who sicked that knight on me simply because I kidnapped some Russian
princess!
I would have won that fight on the Puchai River if that angel hadn't butted in!"
Did the shadow of Zmey, overflowing the altar whisper in your ears,
Of a greater-and necessary-communion with fire that was at your fingertips,
And that for the sake of your health, you should get to it as soon as possible?
Surely, the Lamb, who would smash the heads of all dragons to jelly,
And stamp out all memory of snout/scale/fire/claw/lashing tail from mankind,
The Lamb did not leave you forgiven and renewed, soul steam-cleaned and fresh,
Or smile on your Patriarch who counted this conflict a "holy war"
And conferred his blessing on you.
Did the voice of that Tartar worm Zilant of Lake Kaban speak in support of
Zmey?
"If you are ill, then all the better to turn to fire-yes, we should discuss fire,
When you have left the cathedral-I am not comfortable talking about it here,
But I would speak to you of the burning arrows you possess at hand,
The great ones of steel and cold fire that would leave you a name,
An imperishable name, like the great ones on the earth."
I wonder if for one moment as you stood mass, if you heard, in your heart and
soul,
The soft slither of the face cloth and shroud

as they dropped to the tomb's stone floor,
The aromatic spices and myrrh falling from between the folds,
The harsh grate of stone rolling away, the purposeful pad of the wounded feet
Across the tomb's confines and out into the early morning dark,
Were you moved to imagine any of that-even if it was as hushed and
imperceptible
As a fire skipper lighting on the lantana bush's flower,
or a single raindrop on a pine needle,
I wonder if you grappled with the enormity of the debt that was paid for sin's
wage,
The victory over the grave-Life giving up its Life that all might come to life,
Or did you simply see the overflowing dark from you (and outside you)
Across altar, dome, mosaics and icons of buffeting wings, crooked talon,
Horned heads twining like bunches of wind-kissed summer sunflowers?
What Jesus did you pray to standing there on Easter Eve?
What Jesus approved the stones you rolled into place, the 300 buried in Bucha,
The 900 in Kyiv Oblast-the countless bodies in Mariupol and elsewhere?
What Jesus did you pray to on Easter Eve-which Redeemer heard you,
And whispered forgiving words-sweet
as honeycomb or bird's milk cake-into your ear?
Or was it simply the low, severed cable fizzing speech of a dead dragon,
Slain by the Tartar spear of a Russian knight in the small blood sea
Of Lake Puchai?

AUTUMN'S GUMSHOE

Tapping the sweating mug
In time with the arterial strobe
Of the bar's neon sign
Autumn's gumshoe stares at his reflection
Looking back at him in the window seat pane
Counting the seams and scars through the zig zagging spill
Of autumn night's rain snakes
Shoulder holster hidden beneath his trench coat
Smelling of fresh leather oil
As he does his best to forget the last two cases
Two dames long on moxie but short on life
The alimony payments three months behind
The dog convalescing at his sister's house
And the Repo kid he chased down the block last night
And picture in his booze-soaked mind
The Florida Keys vast quilt of emerald-blue swells
Low scudding cloud white as Cheviot sheep
A scent like Camarones a la Diabla blowing off the waves
And a blond in a yellow top and tight jeans
Mojito in hand shades ringed with sun dogs
Cheering from the transom
As the hooked marlin explodes from the surf
Sword tip and sail bright as a ball of
St. Elmo's Fire

SUMMER'S GUMSHOE

Driven out of his apartment by August's suffocating balm
Snub-nosed revolver and cleaning kit abandoned on the kitchen table
He leans on the fire escape rail
Dressed in baggy cargo shorts and an oversized Hawaiian shirt
Breast-pocket palm dabbed with the three rubies of old blood
Courtesy of his last client's abusive ex
Feeling exhausted as the street's deliquescent elms
He takes in
The day's dying tangelo glow on the shop facades
Listens to the car-horns dogs talking couples laughing and fighting
The bump and thump of food carts
And sees the ex-welterweight champ turned limo driver
With the blue-green food dye goatee and dark sunglasses
Doing his usual Wizards of The Coast card trades
With the Latino boys from the floor above his
But he straightens and comes alert
The late checks from his clients forgotten
Remembering the face on the carton that called him to this biz
When a young girl starts busking on the street corner
Sawing away on her violin strings in a cover
Of Titanium

PASSING THROUGH

Hebrews 13:14
English Standard Version
[14] For here we have no lasting city, but we seek the city that is to come.

If you believe, then yes indeed, you know you're just passing through this world,
Like a jazz quartet, rocked to sleep by a mighty fine line on the way to the next
gig,
The next grand hotel, boarding house,
Air-BNB, dressing-room, back-stage crash-pad,
Instrument cases plastered with tags-trombone, trumpet, drums, bass,
Or shipped ahead in the plane's hold-while you toss and turn in the too little seat,
Dreaming through night-cloud, moonshine, wing-shine over black water,
Through the star-slivered cream of cloud and long-dead light,
Of the good notes, the bad notes, the half-notes, the blue notes of a Life,
The sugar and salt shared with the spirit's upswung scroll of raising or lowering
A tone by a half-step-changes-the bridges, chops, licks and blows of simple living.
You live in the Lord and die in the Lord, and do the best you can,
Because you are always-at your best or worst-in transition,
Moving on-family, job, fatherhood, motherhood, loved or alone,
Traveling players declaiming in sun or
shadow-props heaped outside the storage-unit,
Broadway, off-Broadway, summer stock or park/street improv,
It's just a matter of time-if you know The Son-before the old gig comes to an end,
And you retire your sax, pen, earthmover, carpenter's saw, fisherman's net, mouse,
Before you are upswept-taken up and out by grace's gondola,
To a finer realm-a better reward than the buck and shimmy of rail or altitude,

(one day in heaven America/Syria/Nigeria/Albania/Greece/Russia/UK will be
anecdotes)
The promise of Peace fulfilled-the joy of being in The Presence overwhelming,
Like the rivers-the living rivers-rushing from the base of the throne…

But when it's time to leave (and you know in heaven America will be an
anecdote)
And you exit to catch the Lyft or Uber to the train-station or the airport,
Your red-eyes go wide as you see what happened the night before…

And you see the dried trails of last night's hurled egg-slime in yellow and white
Splashed in dull smears on the windows next to the front door,
The scatological graffiti glyphs-gang names, turf claims on the porch posts,
The empty beer bottles, crushed soft-drink cans and plastic wrappers
In the green grass-shards shining like halite on the walkway,
Piked and worried over by the morning's first murder of crows,
And there's the old landlady beat and defeated slumped on the porch glider,
Tears highlighting the grooves and runnels in her cracked and exhausted features,

Spine bowed, cap of frizzed gray stirred by the low, spring breeze,
the broom and dust pan held loosely in chapped, thin fingers,
Well, what can you say-what can you really say, except…

Yeah, you know you're moving on to a better place,
But it sure hurts to see a decent old boarding house
Treated
This
Way

MOURNING DOVES

The mourning doves lead a charmed life around here
At least in our backyard they certainly do
They pace the walls and even the back patio looking like
Plump bowling pins of brown and gray fat with noblesse
Their eyes as black as olives or American nightshade berries
Bobbing their heads like they are rocking out on earbuds
Enjoying some Mark Knopfler, Gabriel Laboriel or Gabriella Quevedo
As if their lives like those of master criminals or politicians' sons
Are caught in some CD groove of subliminal total grace
Like they have get-out-of-predator's-beak cards hidden in their feathers
I am not kidding around here
The mockingbirds don't go after them neither do the crows
This is red-tailed and red-shouldered hawk county
But nope no takers this duo just cuts the struts and goes where they will
As if to say hey we're paying out major protection money
We're good with the raptors until autumn comes around
That's when we have to renegotiate the payoffs in bugs and birdseed
They just take the long and unfussy mosey
Past the anemic corn stalks and the sun-bleached crow decoy
(really a dark brown more than black in a good light)
And neither the lean mean marmalade or the fat tuxedo cat
Have been able to bag either one of this couple
In the time they have been hanging around our yard
These are two Superb and Unperturbed Squab
I am not sure they would flinch at a grenade lob
They just jackhammer cruise maybe three or four feet

From the pool or my lawn chair and then prissily withdraw
To the milkweed and thistle near the electrical box
As if they meant to come up to me and say
Do you mind if we talk we think we have grand insights
That we must share regarding the deleterious direction
Your life is taking these days and if we could have a moment
Oh no no no sorry our mistake really nothing helpful
To impart sorry to disturb you big mistake
But we'll contact you and do thistle ticks and cracked corn
Sometime

CAMPFIRE

When you come down to it, do we tend a campfire?
Well, fire is fairly frisky and can't be mistaken
For a patient lying in a hospital bed ringing for the nurse,
Asking for more cranberry juice or a changed bedpan or new IV drip,
Or their Kindle with their latest fave;
And it's certainly not a flock of Hampshire sheep
Just waiting for a shepherd to take it to market.
But in the most obvious sense, yes, we tend it: from first flame blaze to ashes,
We feed it, help it along, stamp it out when we are ready
To resign the firepit and go back inside our cabin or tent.
Warmth-literal and figurative is the dividend when we're in the trees in the night:
Familial fun, friendly bon homie, romantic musings, reunions and capers,
Creepy scout tales, the counterpoint for a bard's declaim, a memoriam or reunion,
Catching a wandering guitar or listening
to the measured beat from someone's skins.
Fire's a good backdrop isn't it: for humor, gravity, sloth, emotional healing,
There's an atavistic balm to flame/woodsmoke/moon shadow/woods,
When we are shorn of civilization's props and discontents,
Earbuds, headphones, iphones, smartphones, monitors, mice and Gameboys.
There's a peace in watching wood curl, char and blacken, ghost away,
There's a peace in spring or summer's vegetal ruffle and downshift and shuffle.
That said, then maybe it's the campfire that tends us more than we tend it:
Fire as a ministering, restorative element rather than tinder and ignite,
Light guided through the long night to water/dirt/sand/end,
When the kindling is down to no more than a brittle spinal column
Of ash and red coals like the smoking discs of a small

Meteor-cooked *Compsognathus* under blazing skyscraper ferns and
Boiling crimson and platinum skies and black-belching clouds,
Coals throbbing like a ship's klaxon in time with the breeze,
In time with our tired hearts and torpid blood,
Bright as lynx-eyes flashing red in the headlights sweep,
Isn't that the best part-when dinner, songs and stories are done,
And the night draws in, the temperature drops out, and the orange hunter's
moon,
Plays hide-and-seek with the occasional drifting scow
Of moon-garbed cumulus, and the campsite grows still bit by bit,
Maybe that's when the campfire, like a doctor with a recalcitrant charge,
Kicks in and says *if you let me I can help you out right here*
Between half-sleep and full-sleep, drowsiness and dream,
The right prescription, the right treatment-here it is.
That is when the campfire truly tends us,
When we are down to just the charry rudiments of flame and ash,
The language of leisure and escape is scraped off the day's page to
The explosion of knots, the shift and collapse of crisscrossed tinder,
The syrupy chirrup of crickets and occasional patter of avian chatter,
The passage of unseen wings and crackle of leaf and twig,
The hollow thud of an ice-chest's lid slamming,
And cellophane crinkle of breaking ice,
The sudden gust of laughter and amused whispers,
The muted and far-off jangle of a porch-swing,
While the breeze brings a hint of long-cooled ribs and sauce,
The medicinal scent of eucalyptus and the barest thread of jasmine,
Buttered popcorn, wet dog, detergent, evening primrose, verbena and nicotiana.
When the people lights go and only the occasional flashlight snaps on,
And animal eyes shine from the brush
Like the quick pass of a bike's reflector,
That's when the world in redux is culled to ember's glow,
Stentorian breath, the query that doesn't know where it's going,
The completed punchline for the joke started two hours earlier.
I would say that is when a campfire truly tends us,
When Husbands and wives, young couples and old,
Jab the poker into the logs' leavings, stir the coals,

Fan them anew with wadded pieces of briquet sack,
Scuff the boot sole lightly against the firepit's edge,
Tap the half-melted ice adhering to the top of the soft drink can,
Watching the sparks do their quick up-flung flit and double-helix.
Yes, sometimes a campfire tends us and heals us-that's what I think,
When it's just the two of you, the kids asleep in the cabin,
And the burdens/joys/weariness/pleasures/resentments/triumphs
Fly away like beads of seawater and spume off a whale's fluke before it
Crashes down slips down into deep water
Winking out like the phosphorescent fall of theme park fireworks,
Time and rumination come down to kindling/collapse/flare,
Soughing oak/sibilant wisteria/palette smear of Pleiades,
Heaven's sequined shell spinning overhead.
And that is when you catch each other's eye,
Sitting muffled and mellow in the director's chairs,
Faces sheened by the dwindling flames, craved into fleeting totems,
Immobile, *the thought undone, the memory undone, the love and loss undone,*
And the two of you just smile at each other
And without speaking, cup/can/mug/marshmallow sticker in hand,
You say to yourself *I am content I am just content,*
And the other nods, lips quirking in a lazy grin,
As if to answer back *I am too we will remember this let's remember this,*
Let's keep it in mind when we head back have to go back,
The heavy freight's voice loud as Siri traded out for this,
The resonance of frog-song bird-song bug-song wind-sigh limb-scrape,
Silence profound as cave-chutes or midnight hardpan star-fields
I am content
I am.

PROFILE PICS AND HASHTAGS

Switching social-media profile pics and hashtags
Like remoras trading up on pelagic sharks
Or old hobos scooting from train to train
More people get used to the thin gruel of light loves
And swift hates
Like begging friars settling
For another famishment ration
Of rock and acorn soup.

MORNING PRAYER

We don't always need a raucous caucus
Trombone testimonies and hand-claps
Pentecostal fire frog-glottals of charismatic tongues
Sometimes all the soul needs are spare and simple truths
Nothing more than the economy of
A skinny shaker chair before a second-story window
Three apricots in a dish on the sill
Marriage of sky's sizzling blue and late summer goldenrod
Glassine seas of wind-bent wheat on rolling hills
Sheep-puff shadows of white cumulus
Spun-top dervish drop of lenticular giant
The gilding of gospel by the brief contrapuntal
Of black-capped chickadee wren or junco
Lazy loiter of somnolent honeybee and hornet-fly
On a light-striped page of Luke
Balm in Gilead gleaned from catching the
Crooked periscope of a tortoiseshell's tail
Making its way through tobacco-brown grass
The quietude of a good room and Christ's words
Sometimes that's what the soul needs
Even if there is
No shaker chair
No wheaten ocean
No chickadee song or tortoiseshell's tail

JAPANESE FRIENDSHIP GARDEN OF SAN DIEGO/05/29/22

"SHODO" THE LEGACY OF TRADITIONAL CALLIGRAPHY
CURATED BY BEFU OSAWA

If you could surround yourself each day
With the deep-sea calm
Of calligraphy strokes
These deft characters
Starved to beggars' ribs
And herons' legs
You would forget
Your warrior's dreams

JAPANESE FRIENDSHIP GARDEN OF SAN DIEGO/05/29/22
"SHODO" THE LEGACY OF TRADITIONAL CALLIGRAPHY
CURATED BY BEFU OSAWA

Standing in front of the
Calligraphy chamber's window
Facing the rock garden outside
My mind frees Old Whale's
Scarred head from the stone
As he breaches
Amidst the backs
Of his brothers

PATRIARCH KIRILL OF MOSCOW AND ALL THE RUSSIAS

"Russia has never attacked anyone"
Patriarch Kirill of Moscow and All The Russias
"We have entered into a struggle that has not a physical,
but a metaphysical significance"
Patriarch Kirill of Moscow and All The Russias

When Tsar Ivan the Terrible came to Moscow's cathedral
To celebrate Great Lent on the Sunday of The Veneration of The Cross,
(just before he rode to wage great slaughter against the folk of Novgorod)
He, reeking of massacre and old blood, his *Oprichnina* butchers in tow,
The courageous metropolitan Philip refused to bless him,
(had not Ivan become a "terror to good works" in contravention of Paul's words)
And rebuked him before the congregation for his merciless savagery.
He stood up to him in peril of life, fearless as the Martyr Stephen,
Who cut the hearts of the Sanhedrin with his eloquence and faith.
Metropolitan Philip had no illusions what the Rurik Tsar could do to him,
As wicked and keen-witted as Andronikos Komnenos Ivan was,
But Philip spoke the truth-tabored like a dove amidst the mews of raptors,
Beseeching Ivan to give up the *Oprichnina* terror state,
To pension off his hard-riding, hard-killing band of Jebusite boors.
He sorrowed as much for the state of the Tsar's soul as he did for the slain,
(the sacrifices that Ivan said he "made to Cronos"),
Philip honored the apostles words "to obey God rather than man,"
And to make intercession for those who would feed the sword on the morrow,
The metropolitan's bravery sweeter than bird milk cake or honey mead,

He might as well have been in the Chaldean furnace with the exiles,

That's how strong his confidence in Christ and

his commission was-he gave no shrift,

To the wielders of broom and dog's head who surrounded Rurik's seed,

Even though many churchmen had embraced the *Oprichnina*,

Given up the right to intercede for the oppressed and embraced evil,

Like a mother bird that allowed a strange chick in its nest,

To kill her brood while warming itself at her breast.

Well, where could Philip go when the humanity of the Orthodox Tsar,

No more than the dead light of Venus hundreds of years deferred,

A butter-spread of dead stars in some galaxy's coal sack corner,

Was all but snuffed out: he was as cruel and remorseless as Haman

Who sought the extermination of the Jews residing in Persia's satraps.

After the massacre of Novgorod, when the swords and muskets did their work,

The dead heaped like bulwarks and Archbishop Pimen degraded,

Philip was deposed and imprisoned: first in the Theophany Monastery,

Then transferred to the Monastery of The Fathers in Tver,

Strangled in his cell by order of the blood-glutted Tsar who could not forgive him

For his rebuke and Christlike example of selfless intercession.

Philip emptied himself out as the Don empties itself into the Sea of Azov,

Like the lamb before the shearers he had faced the end,

Sensing his fate, had asked for communion three days before his death,

Surely his soul shone like the white bearded iris in its leaving,

Pure as a winter marten gamboling in the snow drifts,

When it was taken up into heaven and the bosom of our Lord.

The shepherd who exercises his pastoral staff is a glory to God,

The one who recovers a lamb from the mouth of the evening wolf,

Is a true servant, and wins the ivy bound chaplet of eternal life:

Are they not fixed to Salvation with the nails of love and sacrifice?

So, what of you, Patriarch Kirill of Moscow and All the Russias?

Tell us: why did you not speak in the cause of Life and Righteousness,

Raise yourself up and roar as the winter bear rising in green spring?

Why did the words for Peace that should have flown like the albatross

Over the moiled waves, remain unspoken, restrained and reproved?

When the Russian President resolved to deprive a free people of their sovereignty,

Why did you not proffer the myrtle and olive leaves of mercy,

Why did you not raise up the cross-the sign of the Author of Life,
And intercede as the Martyr Philip or Archbishop Pimen of Novgorod did,
Counting their lives less than a mizzle of evening dew-a spatter of spring rain,
And remind the Russian President that all who pursue wars of aggression,
Go down with their pomp, their viols and armies to a couch of worms?
Recall the priest Abiathar and his fellows who were put to death,
When Abiathar rose up in defense of the blameless David before the rage of
Saul?
Your words of violence were adamantine-unbreakable as titanium,
As when the prophet Hosea called to account the bands of priests
Who murdered on the way to Shechem, were you not as one of them,
When you approved the harrowing of cities and the spilling of blood?
You went with the destroyer as happily as the Levite priest when the
Sons of Dan took him and the teraphim out of Micah's house!
Repent and remember mercy and compassion: how a Good Shepherd
Defends the weak and helpless, vigilant among the sheep folds and sheepcotes,
Ready to drive the wolf and bear away from the ewes and lambs,
Taut as the bowstring turning the foes of his flock.
Will you not remember what you were called to do?
Will you not hear the bells of Mariupol, Kyiv and Kharkov?
Will you not meet the old men's eyes of the children of Mariupol,
Kyiv and Kharkov?
Will you not look upon the bombed out hospitals and theaters?
The Prophet Daniel and the Apostle Peter obeyed God before Man,
They did not fear the judgment of kings, authorities and potentates.
Listen to your conscience in the long night and early morning hours:
Is it a foghorn all but blotted out by night billows?
Is it a cricket's chirp from behind a fridge or the baying of an oil-patch dog?
Is it the tick of water from the icicles under the eaves on to a bed of firs needles?
Pray to the Lord for the resolve and courage of the Metropolitan Philip,
Remind your President of Ezekiel's lament for the Prince of Tyre,
Remind him there is one who can kill the soul and the body.
For your own sake, consider Philip and Abiathar or
Ambrose, the Bishop of Milan, who did not quail from laying penance
On the Roman Emperor Theodosius when he allowed his troops
To massacre the innocent as well as guilty in the Hippodrome,

When the Thessalonian rebels murdered the imperial garrison captain Botheric.
Bareheaded and in sackcloth, Theodosius repented his actions.
One day, you will appear like the rest of us before the Lord,
Soul quivering in the air-tiny as the bee hummingbird or goldcrest,
The outworn dross of ego and self-importance shucked like corn husk.
Tell me, when He asks why you called the Ukraine War a Holy War,
And why you did not intercede for the victims and your own people
Who never wanted to see their sons and daughters deployed against those people,
Who knew a wrongful conflict when they saw it,
Will you tell Him, The Judge of All: "We have entered into a struggle,
That has not a physical, but a metaphysical significance"?
Will you excuse yourself, saying that it was a needed response
To the evils of "excess capitalism and homosexuality"?
And will the eyes of the dead of Bucha, Borodianka and Staryi Bykiv
Creep toward you on that day
With the slow and inexorable advance
Of an ice wave on the shore of Lake Baikal?

WINTER'S GUMSHOE

"We have all been here before"
Wakes up to pain's semaphore: dried stickiness at the back of his skull,
Cramped limbs/jouncing motion/uphill grade, broken nose taking in
Stale body sweat, miasma of piled gas-rags, musty moving pads, fir and pine scent.
Blackened eyes adjust to five finger beams of moon silver phosphor
Streaming through bullet-holes in the buckled trunk's top,
Casting baby-spots on blood's black spatter on wadded trench coat's front.
Feels the bone-chilling cold of car's undercarriage braces legs as car shimmies
And bucks up mountain road-fir and pine scent thickening,
Sidewalls spinning through mountain road's mire of ice and slush
Not surprised when frozen hand fumbles and finds shoulder-holster filched.
Memory shards like sputtering roadside flares take him back to the shadow
Jumping up from the side of the midnight midway's concession booth
Blackjack swinging down while the bling buried dwarf cackles
And bounces from his seat on the merry-go-round's hacked and peeling horse.
Registers low laughter from the front seat and lets hate's black treacle
Have its way isotope poison and honey squeezed from the hexagon
And slowly ever slowly barely breathing moves his hand to his belt
Slides underneath to withdraw the small stabbing blade from belt sheath
And fold it into his palm planning the strike when the trunk opens
And one of them reaches down to pull him out
Passing his Ruger to the other before bending down
Exposing face chin neck throat in moon wash and drifting snow
Thoughts cold as the car's undercarriage he smiles and waits,
The Night as Catalyst's history coming back to him bit by bit

Like an outraged client fanning incriminating photos in a card spread.
And as he waits as he waits barely breathing
He calls up the dream of emerald-blue swells
Boiling blue sky scudding cloud white as Cheviot sheep
The blond in tight jeans and yellow top
Standing in front of the boat's transom
Shades ringed with sun dogs Mojito in hand
Hair whipping backwards like a windsock on a small runway
A scent like Camarones la Diabla blowing off the waves
While he waits, buckled into his seat for the marlin to take the hook.
Yes, they will take the hook.
Then face chin neck throat in moon wash and drifting snow
Uncoiling from the trunk and going for the second one.
And after a long while, they came to a stop.

MAENADS

She bragged, yes she did: the Democratic congresswoman from New York
About helping to stop a bill bolstering security for the Supreme Court Justices
And their families-she preened, preened like a pink and white cockatoo,
Fluffing its crest, spreading its wings and walking the perch.
She did this after the arrest of the man planning
the assassination of Justice Kavanaugh
And his family (the would-be killer cried off and called 911 instead).
The murderous imbroglio was over Roe versus Wade, of course,
But the Democratic congresswoman exulted over her deed on social-media
Like a gladiator in a fish-masked bronze Thracian helmet,
Drunk on the applause and plaudits of the toga set, moon-walking the arena
sands,
Brandishing their bloody gladius in victory, armored arm bedight in western light,
Or some Polish hussar, his back-wing crest of raptor feathers fluttering
While he rears his steed of war over a mound of fallen Turkish janissaries.
The man who planned to kill the justice and his wife and children
Had a suitcase containing a Glock 17 pistol, ammunition, a knife,
Tactical gear, pepper spray, zip ties, a hammer, a screwdriver and duct tape.
It made no difference to the Democratic congresswoman from New York,
It made no difference to AOC who voted No on beefing up security.
And the Speaker of The House, Nancy Pelosi, said the justices were protected,
Why should we add one precaution more?
And I thought once again: here we are living in Dragons Days,
Troubled hours of adamantine scales and fiery snout,
Where love and kindness are scarce as baby formula,
But demon motivation and recreation, is at an all-time high.

What shall we say to the women who cheered AOC's vote to withhold
protection?
Woe to violent (women we will say women) reclining on couches of ivory,
Joining ivory couch to ivory couch and mouse to mouse,
Wearing jaguar masks to zoom-room chats, trading recipes for bat goulash.
Was she sorry (AOC), was she disappointed that the assassin had lost his nerve?
Did she and the Ruth's loveless Sisters (no nuns or nurses be they no not at all)
When he turned himself in, did they drum their heels and slap their screens?
Did they shriek in frustrated rage that the inside of the Kavanaugh home
Wasn't red as a halved pomegranate, the front yard cordoned off with yellow tape,
No milling blue, no flashing visibars of police cars,
No press vans-and no sheet-covered lumps hurried out to
The backs of ambulances-were they sorry that didn't come to pass?
Do we live in times when wild women with bloody nails go roving
In the streets and in the squares, to seek the one their soul hates;
Will the watchmen find them as they go about the city,
And will they step aside when wild women with bloody nails
With disordered locks and eyes like hawks, mouths like commodes,
Say to them, raking faces and gnashing tooth to tooth,
"We will descant to one another about Our Truth,
Will you tear-gas us in the city's gate, or let us go and seek a prey,
For we will go about the streets and squares to find the one our soul hates,
And curse our worst and wounding curse for all the sweet and airy wombs,
While we crochet and bay like dogs amidst the grave and marble tombs!"
She bragged, yes she did: the Democratic Congresswoman from New York,
(they hagged and preened and streamed their stream of jungle dreams)
(of bloody ferns and gaining jaws and frisking spears/abortion's cause)
(of justices in ragged robes run to ground on boatless shores and bloody coves)
And I wonder still: did she, her heart cold as autumn's starry canopy,
Pray that the next attempt succeed and soon: some judge's wife or child,
Face down in the entry, in the family room, laid out in the kitchen,
Outside the school, in the super-market, in an elm and willow shaded park?
What is this Right that you are fighting for-the right to fill a Spartan gorge,
To line the walls of Jericho once more with murdered babes in pots and urns,
What is this right that you are fighting for that blanches you of motherhood,
Your gender's (will you assume that they are women do you presume?) virtues,

And all that is in womankind,
nurturing (you assume you presume) and reckoned good,
In what bacchanal of dragon dance and stellar wine,
Did you learn to banish love and pity, and gird your loins with hemlock leaves,
To weave deadly nightshade around your vitiated dugs,
What is this right you're fighting for-to fill a yawning Spartan gorge?
Remember the frenzied Thracian women-the Maenads-who tore Orpheus apart,
That incomparable musician and son of Appollo and Kalliope,
Because of his fidelity to the memory of Eurydice,
When he refused to entertain them with the fire from his inestimable lyre?
Those women were called "the raving ones," were inspired by Dionysus,
Zeus' son and the patron of wine and madness,
To enter into a state of ecstasy through intoxication and dancing,
Executing that god's strange rites-violent women forming gangs!
Our new maenads won't don a fox-skin in the streets,
Helmets with bull horns on their liquored, tossed, disordered tress,
Or brandish staffs of twining ivy, capped with pinecones…
But they are here.
Oh yes, they are here.

CORMORANT

When I am taking a walk at one of the local parks
And I see the thin zig-zag of the blue-black cormorant
Sitting stock still on a thrust of lake branch
Cruel beak questing upwards
I think to myself that God took a fingernail
Blackened with the leftover soot of an erring soul
To scribe some dark and enduring truth
On the golden palimpsest of our bright and fragrant days

06/24/22

Then this happened today
It happened today (The Decision)
And it was like…
Like the light of a spelunker's lost helmet snapping on in the dark,
From its bed of chalk ground bone and dust,
Strafing the long throat of a cave's chimney chute,
Driving the bat dance back to its stalactite curtain
Of guano lava peat sand and sinter,
Something gold and amber giving forth,
Stuttering snapping back on staying on.
Like walking through a war-hammered cityscape
Of fuming steel crumbled stone and drifting ash,
And seeing the Ukrainian girl in red formal dress
Going through graduation solemnities with her classmates
In the ruins of their school in spite of the distant chatter,
Of gunfire and percussion of tank shells and serial bombardment,
Her sea-green eyes steady seeing a future that there's a future
Like well water unlocked from the earth's bad skin,
Upwelling silver/blue/gold/white sun-swung,
Leaping, purling, upwelling from groaning loam's checkerboard
Of alkali and dirt death going damp,
The drowsing rod's point forgotten as dust-blanched hands plunge
To grab it scoop it up the bounty red-doubling and bubbling,
Mouths sand-packed cotton-dry taking everything they can
Laughter and weeping increasing with moisture's seeping,
Like some astute street preacher warming his hands around his coffee

Seeing the young man in the grime-crusted hoodie
Float out from the alleyway head down hand going out
For the woman's purse strap the other hand going into his pocket
But the preacher interposes himself, coffee shifted,
And says Brother why don't we duck into the diner and talk,
Come with me take the hand out of the pocket and let's talk,
And the thief's shoulders hitching with sobs,
The man turning him around out of the flow of pedestrians
Out of the sludge stream crawl of old life's desperation.
Like a mother and father called out of exhaustion's sleep
By sometime interstice of grace between shades of night and night,
Sleep-gummed eyes going wide going wider jaws dropping,
Tears streaming down their cheeks, chairs falling over, forgotten,
As they register their daughter sitting up straight in her hospital bed,
Lucent gaze on the flutter of pigeon wing outside the room's window
As she slowly says Mom, Dad, the blue car and my bike,
Is the blue car and my bike-the blue car and my bike over
While broken light and whirring wing shadow roll across the sheets.
Like a lunatic's prisoner tearing out of a double-wide hell
Into morning's sun and shade stipple, duct tape trailing from their wrists and
shins,
Gaining the road beyond a ragged screen of trees and burdock
Flagging down the first car arms outstretched scot free in the bright
Tires screeching rubber scarring blacktop with auto stop
Bird song sun bird song sun and life song loud as winter reveille,
All out in the open sun wheeling overhead all out in the light
Just a concerned voice repeating over and over are you okay?
Well, that's what it feels reading the decision
Something gone right some open door of angel-fire flung open
Some twist of finer frequency and sight that coming together
When so much has been going so wrong
Oh God thank you thank you thank you

WARTIME

It feels like that now wartime a catch in the breath the smothered cough
The too-loud crunch of boot soles across gravel in those moments,
Breath-plumes likes cherry vapes or ghost jellies in front of helmets and goggles,
Someone trading someone else a photo a text a love text a hate text a promise,
Tapping a full magazine against the helmet's camo dome,
Before life's fusty truths of armored file movement and muzzle take over,
Moments between crepuscular blue yields to dawn's first pink flush,
Before the immersive gold joins with east's mountain caul of crimson,
Red bonding with veins of platinum-fine as a mead-hall maiden's braids,
Before the bellies of the morning's buttermilk clouds change to bronze,
Before the engines of troop transports and tanks cough and rumble into life,
Like bears coming out of hibernation bearing bad dreams in their jaws,
Before the big lights browed by green/dun/sand snap on like miniature suns,
Sending up roiling cyclones of whirring wing and tiny carapace,
Making the birds swallow their songs like troubadours swallowing rotten walnuts,
Instead of the promised choice chop, rabbit stew and greens-coins for a chanson.
It is like the air in the upper reaches of a room–a drumming of dust/molecule,
Before the argument breaks–before the words are said that cannot be unsaid,
The quick-lightning accusations that no apology amends,
The bilious green connections of a mindset of cyclone sky,
Before porch and shingle, child and dog are scooped up/lifted away,
The meeting of southern cold fronts and eastern warm fronts.
It feels liked that–wartime a catch in the breath the smothered cough
The too-loud crunch of boot soles across gravel and tarmac,
The air-force pilot in his bone-dome watching rain-snakes slice his canopy,
Waiting for the black clouds clour to abate.

It is like hearing the swift, near-silent *chink* of five smooth stones in a sling,
Before the weaver-beam spear's head slaps against a burnished shield.
That's what it feels like: suspiration before the roil of roll-out/tread and steel,
Before the hardening of caustic cocktails of concrete,
Before the bricks are piled up in the backseat, the doxed home lists shared out,
Before the tomato red robes and white bonnets are passed around.
Before the last thread of a trench's violin music trails out with the first weave
Of yellow gas pumping through the concertina strands,
We wonder: how far will we go and when will it end?
Will it end?

THE PRESIDENT'S SON

Romans 7:15-20
English Standard Version

[15] For I do not understand my own actions. For I do not do what I want, but I do the very thing I hate. [16] Now if I do what I do not want, I agree with the law, that it is good. [17] So now it is no longer I who do it, but sin that dwells within me. [18] For I know that nothing good dwells in me, that is, in my flesh. For I have the desire to do what is right, but not the ability to carry it out. [19] For I do not do the good I want, but the evil I do not want is what I keep on doing. [20] Now if I do what I do not want, it is no longer I who do it, but sin that dwells within me.

And compassion, as fragile as a single green shoot in an alkali desert,
Or a brief window of rose and platinum amidst a long bison march of dark cloud,
Impinged, won out for a nonce inside me as I watched the 4chan footage of
The President's Son as he filmed himself weighing those white piles
On a small portable scale-the latter's lit readings going back and forth
Between 20.7 grams and 20.8 before stopping at 20.7 and in that interstice
Between anger and horror, I considered the terrible measure of things,
The weight of addiction-wafer-thin as a fleeting hope but heavy as tungsten,
Those scattered bits and pieces resembling shattered tooth enamel,
Or something culled from a bag of Japanese trail mix,
So small, but capable of destroying health, judgment, family-every good gift.
I marked the hag-ridden, scruffy face with the drooping cigarette
("Two point 0 seven without the bag," that's what The President's Son said)
And thought with sorrow frayed as a suspension bridge's ropes,
How charmed life, privilege and power shorn of every consequence and obstacle,

Is no more than a crumb toss to a moil of black swans in a junkyard sump,
How nothing could suffice a soul hungry and poisonous as a landfill's pit,
How so little (20.7 to 20/8 grams)
could produce the extinguishing of dignity and will,
And set self-respect sidling, punch-drunk and bleary-eyed like a lab assistant
Navigating his or her way past screaming banks of primate cages,
Can be gotten away for so little counted as so much.
Watching The President's Son go about his horrible film work,
I ruminated on the fatal imparities of maladjusted weights and scales,
That each person in this life, with unerring selfishness and complacency,
Measures out and doctors, forsaking opportunities for love, grace and redemption.
And I reflected on the bartering of all that was decent,
meaningful and purposeful,
For solids/reduced to liquid/the miserable marriage of fire, rock, water and pipe.
And how we are all, but for the mercies of God,
His undeserved loving kindnesses,
In danger of small falls and great calamities and a thousand wretched seductions.
("Two point 0 seven without the bag," that's what The President's Son said)
Here is hell doled out in increments,
like bits of bad ice chipped from the walls of Dis,
And I felt a nano-chip or two of pity for the President's awful Son,
Pity thin as a sliver of a sliver of bone missed in an Amazon piranha boil,
Pity slender and fine as a single filament of an orb weaver's web as I saw him,
Blow-torched down to the gaunt lineaments of need and hunger,
Correcting the woman (off-camera) in his hotel room on the junk's final total.
And I wondered: how many people in your life offered to spit in your blind eyes
And tell you to wash in the Pool of Siloam that you might see again,
That would have had you on your feet, glorifying God and His infinite mercy,
How many begged you not to let it come to this not to let it come to this?
I wanted to take you to the Gerasenes country where The Man from Galilee
Healed the demented soul with the demon legion-that
breaker of chains and shackles,
The tomb-crawler, the self-cutter, the howler hiding in the long grave grass
(are we not to some degree howlers hiding in the grave grass even us)
That no one in the area could overpower and restrain.
I never fail to be moved by that particular account laid down in the gospels,

How Christ wiped those devils away like ashes flicked from a shirt's sleeve,

And how that unfortunate, rescued from possession, glorified God,

Praising all that the Son of Man had done for him.

But then my mind returned to your laptop-the Pandora's box pending,

And I speculated on whatever other horrors were waiting to emerge,

Like bone-faced hatchetfish and anglers out the lightless muck of an abyssal sea,

Monsters meted out in smoking shades of shining mercury and chrome,

Lurching out of the dark with pop-eyes, underslung jaws and tinsel teeth.

What would we learn of your moon and night-soil trysts with China and Russia?

Ultimately, what would it cost to keep it mum and bail you out?

What iron hand in an iron glove would close around the neck of an honest judge?

And I wondered when it was all played out,

who would pay, who would just give up,

Who would roll over and surrender to riptide and fog, needle and nostrum,

Break down before the terrible imparity of maladjusted scales and weights,

Bartering all that was decent, meaningful, purposeful in their lives,

For solids/reduced to liquid/the miserable marriage of fire, rock, water and pipe,

For the bottle, for the packet, for the prescription bottle (and unprescribed),

("Two point 0 seven without the bag," that's what someone's daughter or son said)

What lives would be blasted into splinters and shards like space trash

Bouncing and caroming against the panels of a derelict satellite,

How could anyone forgive you anymore than a mama bird could forgive

The honeyguide or common cuckoo that puts it eggs in their nests

So that when they hatch and get the food while the mother's chicks starve?

And yet some thread of pity as slender as the possibility of a tumor's remission,

As imperceptible as a snatch of thrush song between the blasts of bombing runs,

Remained, even for The President's Son went descanting on weights and measures,

The shaky camera going from the scale on the dresser to the skivvies on the floor,

Dumped on the hotel room's floor-a mishmash

of shucked off cloth and scattered shoes.

I reminded myself of the God who could forgive the Assyrians of Nineveh,

The forgiveness of Esau for his brother who had stolen his birthright,

The times God showed mercy towards Israel as it wandered the wilderness,

Jesus' forgiveness of the woman caught in adultery,

The Son of God in extremis,

pleading for The Father to pardon those who crucified Him,

And the Martyr Stephen asking the same as he sunk under the hail of stones.

And I found myself hoping the same for The President's troubled Son,

And I remembered the line from a Rainer Maria Rilke poem,

How all the dragons in our lives are princesses waiting for us to act,

Just once, with beauty and courage-yes,

those words came to me as I watched the film.

Again, I wanted to take him back to the Gerasenes country, point at the man,

Free of possession and say, ask him how he was freed-like a trafficked African cat

Out of a gangster's two-penny zoo-by the Man from Galilee.

And I saw myself-all of us to some degree-transgressions minor and major,

Crouching like savages in a forest clearing of mist-shiny giants,

Suddenly waking up in the crosshatch of dawn's rose and platinum beams,

Hunter's bow in one hand, burdened with back quiver filled with arrows,

Dressed in ragged wolfskins, helmed with a moth-eaten bearskin cap,

Skin shellacked with the camo of mud and sap, bare feet dug into leaf carpet,

Staring in shock at the arrow in the breast of a dead white hart,

Splayed before us, one hoof feebly kicking

the tentative tendrils of woods' mist to pieces,

Winter blue eyes bright as topaz rolling in death-terror,

antlers making a light trench in humus,

And there a golden crown and collar and chain rattling from its throat,

From about its throat-as we shake our heads in stunned dismay and innocence,

Saying to ourselves, I never shot this, I never released the arrow, I know I did not.

I would never have killed anything so beautiful and pure.

How could this be-how could I wake to responsibility for this atrocity?

And then, out of the brindled reaches of the emperor-oaks, pines and larches,

A voice like a calm good green wind fills our heads and says:

You do, every day, and I forgive you because you are mine and I will forgive you.

But as you thank me for that, and address your plaints to me, I ask you to do this:

Pray for The President's Son-and his father-that they turn to me,

For they need it as much as you.

LITTLE COFFINS

When the vaccinated go into paroxysms of withering keyboard rage
And holy indignation (selfish you are selfish you will kill us all)
Because you question the efficacy and safety of experimental jabs,
Coming at you on social-media like a snorting rodeo bull that just bucked you off,
Storming at you like a coach from the dug-out, eyes transformed
Into spinning red pinwheels of hate, right cheek bulging with chaw,
Huffing to the mound because you just pitched a homer with three men on,
What you want to say to them with the ineffable and grave tenderness of
An old man humming his dying guide dog to its rest in the vet's room,
In tones soft and delicate as the stirring of breeze-bent reeds
At the edge of a moon-silvered lake
Is this:
For the first time in 30 years there is a high demand
For children's coffins in Canada.

JOE BOLGER/RED TRUCK

What you wouldn't give when you are weighed down by this world,
To be able to just sit in the driver seat of a gently rusting red pick-up,
Like the kind you find in one of Joe Bolger oil paintings,
Parked at the edge of equally rubrous sorghum or glassine wheat,
Green grass threaded with yellow thistle undulant and bendy with the wind,
Like the keys of a concert grand worked from ascending G to descending C,
The green tips catching the flint bits and sun-spackle of autumn's russet light.
The reason you are sitting out here is that *she* is making dinner,
And you don't want to disturb her while she is making dinner,
You just want to watch the day wind down and the dark take the fields.
It would be a joy to just recline and listen to some cool jazz or swing dialed low,
Tapping the steering-wheel, watching the dark take through the rows
Snake through the rows like a congregation of congers,
Feeling the sweat-pops cool on the brow while on a distant hill,
The roof of a vermiculated barn dipped in foundry's molten gold,
Semaphores and helixes in time with the radio's beat,
Hoppers back-flipping and ticking off the cooling hood,
While crows complain in rusty rancor about the day's proceeds,
While whippoorwills add their soothing descants.
And there is something about a dream about a dinner you want to remember.
Then there's luxury of closing one's eyes and taking a deep breath
Of the soul's reviving whiff of apple orchard and pear's windfall,
The ghost of a good porter or stout on the tongue,
As someone lays down a fine wail on a tenor sax or trumpet solo,
(And you picture sitting with her in a dark club somewhere in Europe)
As the armored clouds, thick as pangolin scales,

Lark and spark far off over the northern hills, still a good way yet,
Grumbling like old men in a nursing home arguing over cards.
And there was something about a storm in the dream about dinner,
The one that woke you this morning when the two of you were in bed.
What a joy to sink into the driver seat upholstery like a stingray,
Slipping with grace into a sand bed in clear turquoise water,
To watch the birds zip back and forth over the fields like darning needles
Stitching song/warble/trill into the day's growing wound of scarlet and mauve,
To return the stare of a marmalade-colored barn cat when it hops a fence post,
Ostentatiously licking a paw, chatoyant pupils showing glints of ingot's blaze.
And then, on queue: the syrup-thick chirrup of field crickets,
And the arguments of children from the farmhouse at your back.
There's joy untrammeled: easing into the staid bellows of stentorian breathing
While God's Green Machine ticks down like the engine of your red pick-up,
Listening to the whisper of grass and thistle scrape against bumper and hubs,
While the congers between the field rows turns into a thick licorice pour.
Turning your head, drowsy with music when you feel the prickle of forearm,
As a ladybug makes its way across the arm thrown over the driver side window,
Lazily making its way through follicle and sunburnt, age-spotted skin,
Before it opens its red wings-not as rust-red as your truck-and before it can fly,
It is flicked away-wind-spun with the sudden gust from the north,
Along with the young hoppers and lacewings crawling over the glass.
It is at time like that-on the cusp of the Magic Hour-that it seems,
Like the soul is skipping over river fords of empyrean light,
And the days burdens twist away like crappie or catfish on a stringer,
In calm, green water under a shady bivouac of shore willows.
As your eyelids lower like blinds pulled halfway down,
You hear the delighted screams of the girls riding their ponies at the next farm,
And you pray that there will always be pony rides for young girls,
Waterhole meets, and boys hazing dogs in summer grass at sunset,
Tire swings hanging from old oak, maple, hornbeam and beech.
Then maybe-just maybe-as mauve and grayish blue dismiss
The last of the sun's dimming arc of orange and red from the hill tops,
Making the blue irises glow like a huskies' eyes,
Something-in between a chord or half-note on the radio
And the muffled clatter of a big spoon in the kitchen sink,

The dream unfolds like a flower-releasing memory like an angry bee.

You remember how you once surprised her with a kiss on the throat,

As she was about to peel potatoes in front of the small open window,

The day humid-the air pressurized and laced with ozone,

Dreadnaughts of indigo and rose casting shadows on the rows outside,

The alb of her grackle-shiny black hair smelling clean as creek water,

And how she turned, lips quirked in humor, to meet your kiss.

And in that moment as the eyelids twitch and the wheel-hand goes slack,

The music becomes no more than an aural dusting of powdered sugar

And consciousness and spirit twist together like crappie and cat on their stringer,

A strong current taking away the calm of Tonka green water and willow shade,

Threatening to tear the stringer out of the bank and send it downstream,

Piscine eyes disappearing into water and mud flecked with fool's gold,

Even as the ghost of the kiss publishes itself on your mouth,

And the smell of clean water/apple/peach becomes overpowering,

The dream blows away into pieces like scattered playbills in bus wake,

A hobo's deserted bindle flung from the rails by a train's passing,

A single though impinges with the dream's death:

A man can never really be alone.

A man can never really be alone-for good or ill he can't.

That's when you come awake, hear the small feet crunching through the grass,

Feel the small hand graze your shoulder

and catch the pearlescent voice's soft intone,

Faintly proud and not a little self-important at being trusted with this errand:

"Daddy, mom says to tell you that dinner is ready, and you should come in now."

SELFIE

Stupidity
Profound
As snowfields
Ghost breath of caribou
Squall of antlers
Dipped
In winter foxfire
Of
Northern Lights
The young woman
On the hiking path
Frozen in terror
Like her friend
But
Raising an arm
To take a selfie
Of the standing bear
Leaning in to
Snuffle her hair

SPRING'S GUMSHOE

Is walking briskly past the boat slips, the ghost of a smile quirking his lips,
Striding-with only the hint of a limp-into the hammerfall of early morning heat,
Catching the scent of Camarones a la Diabla coming off the silver-haired waves,
Overriding the sharp smells of boat diesel, bait, fish,
fried food, beer suds, sunscreen,
Garbage, the cloying floral/fruit scents of lotions and aftershave, sea-salt,
As he threads his way through the early morning crush to the end of the marina,
Heading for the boat, a lifetime of exhaustion falling away,
Like a man coming out of a three-day drunk on hardpan,
Cresting a dune to find highway ribbon and
the shot-pocked sign of a greasy spoon
On the roadside.
His smile widens into a grin
As he pictures the homeless Seminole man dressed in plastic bags
Accepting the proffered trench coat and fedora with ecstatic joy,
His face-cheeks sprinkled with the coaldust
of blackheads-breaking into a reveille,
As if, instead of a simple offering of clothes he had engifted the man
With a staff blazing with the welding-torch force of the Pentecostal fire,
Or the coruscant tail of the mythological salamander
spitting like a Roman candle,
The man's wild, improvised jig clearing the sun-warmed sidewalk squares
The orange tribal spider on his gold hair queue flashing in the Florida sun,
Gulls and pigeons lifting into the glister of early morning rays,
As he danced away, the trench coat's belt flailing behind him
Like 4th of July bunting in a strong wind.

He grins again as he remembers the office contretemps when he quit

He sees the fuzzy caterpillar moustache (half-white half-black)

Of his dyspeptic boss quivering in anger and disbelief

As he silently strolls into the back-office rented from Felderman's Novelty Shop,

To drop his private dick's license, gun and holster on the desk,

Throwing an ironic salute to the three-day old brew in the coffeemaker

Before turning on his heel as his boss

sends up a snowfall of incriminating photos,

Old files, fast food wrappers and bags, payroll information,

Now here he is-done with the work/done with the pain,

Mind juking away like a bear from an old lab's blather

From memories of long tails, dead-end leads, furtive naps in decrepit cars,

Listening to rain sizzle like the police-bandwidth,

Camera/Smart Phone crouch beneath motel windows, illicit recordings,

Printing up the fake aliases, identification cards, security clearances,

Standing under elm/oak/magnolia at night outside some quack doctor's office,

Sidling through the rows of crates in abandoned warehouses,

Unlocking cell after cell with a jimmy after being jailed by a sheriff on the take,

Meeting the loosed pit-bull/rottweiler/German shepherd's teeth

With the wadded-up jacket around one arm the hypo needle in the other hand,

The fire in eyes angry gyre of a dame going for a gun/knife/icepick mid-kiss,

The avuncular art-dealer coming up with the knife from its wrist-sheath,

The cousin who called him in to investigate *her* death going for the taser,

Hidden beneath the hasty mounds of coral hay,

The kiss-offs/rationalizations of stooges/offered bribes/

out and out lies/half-truths,

The betrayals/back-stabs/infidelities

of precinct contacts when the big money weighed in,

Was there ever going to be an end to it?

Was there ever going to be an end to it?

Would it all go on like the planet serenely spinning on its axis

But as he passes the crafts and cruisers bustling with activity

Nautical flags starboard spreaders/ensigns/burgees/private signals/courtesy signals

Rippling/soaring/fluttering/snapping/coming in/going out

Cordage and masts creaking/music pumping/couples kissing in the wheel-house

Young people breaking out the brews/a black and

white terrier yapping at the stern
He no longer sees the ghost of the Colonel's autistic son
Whom he failed to save standing in the bow and stern
His spiderman pajamas reduced to earth and moss-spattered rags
Or the young blind woman who found the bagged fentanyl
In her Senator husband's secret closet compartment
He doesn't see her there either auburn hair dusted with coruscating glass shards
From the window she fell back through
When the trade of gunfire startled her into jumping back
But there was The One he saved
And the One who Saved him
That seals the past like the grate of a zipper on a black body bag
Under sizzling cerulean blue and a single cirrus cloud like a bent back centipede,
Ghosts are laid to rest/failure to save forgotten/forgiveness found for self,
The old life shed like a trench coat and fedora left to the hand of a homeless
Seminole man a or a bag of ill-gotten gangster gain redeemed in war,
Handed over to a struggling soup-kitchen saint,
Before the last bill comes due,
Hidden gold left on the doorstep of the storm-battered orphanage.
He scans the marina again but there is no Colonel's autistic son
No blind woman no child's grin-split face on the milk cartoon side
Then here's the last boat slip
And waiting for him
Holding the rod and reel
The blonde in the yellow dress
God hair swirling in the slipstream of crafts
Brown eyes shining with love
Smile sweet as port wine

JAPANESE BEETLES

Buzzing about the clutches of yellow-red fruit
Hanging from my neighbor's guava trees
Lighting, leaving and coming back again
Like impatient heirs
Standing death-watch
On some rich relative
Frustrated by an unwanted climb in vital signs
Ducking out into the antiseptic hallways then returning
Hoping for the worst
Japanese beetles.

FATHERS/HEZEKIAH

Hezekiah and the Babylonian Envoys

¹²At that time Merodach-baladan the son of Baladan, king of Babylon, sent envoys with letters and a present to Hezekiah, for he heard that Hezekiah had been sick. ¹³And Hezekiah welcomed them, and he showed them all his treasure house, the silver, the gold, the spices, the precious oil, his armory, all that was found in his storehouses. There was nothing in his house or in all his realm that Hezekiah did not show them. ¹⁴Then Isaiah the prophet came to King Hezekiah, and said to him, "What did these men say? And from where did they come to you?" And Hezekiah said, "They have come from a far country, from Babylon." ¹⁵He said, "What have they seen in your house?" And Hezekiah answered, "They have seen all that is in my house; there is nothing in my storehouses that I did not show them."

¹⁶Then Isaiah said to Hezekiah, "Hear the word of the Lord: ¹⁷Behold, the days are coming, when all that is in your house, and that which your fathers have stored up till this day, shall be carried to Babylon. Nothing shall be left, says the Lord. ¹⁸And some of your own sons, who will come from you, whom you will father, shall be taken away, and they shall be eunuchs in the palace of the king of Babylon." ¹⁹Then Hezekiah said to Isaiah, "The word of the Lord that you have spoken is good." For he thought, "Why not, if there will be peace and security in my days?"

Long after the Babylonian envoys had left the king of Judah's storeroom,
Dragging themselves away from the stuff like men fighting a riptide's pull,
Their eyes big as the slow lorises or desert ostriches,
Thoughts exploding like mini supernovas, skull's klaxon craving parchment roll
For computations for transportable wealth and siege-logistics

Heads wagging back and forth like box-cedars in a strong breeze,
Their whispers and muted teeth clicking quiet as a heron touching down on a reed mat,
Or the strummed string of a kinnor by the passing flank of a fat tom cat,
Did Hezekiah stay behind, mulling over the vagaries of restoration and loss?
After they were good and gone-and the prophet who had promised castration and servitude
For his heirs had left the palace, mission accomplished, horrors described,
How did Hezekiah feel as he stood there, wrapped in gem burnish and spice scent?
Did the bluff words taste as sour as sumac sauce on his tongue as he considered
Disasters deferred (why not, if there will be peace and security in my days),
Against the terrible fates that awaited his princes several years removed?
(but there will be peace and security in my days).
How does a father (any father), raised from the invalid's bed, king or no,
Write his children off so callously?
Did he see them as young eagle chicks with white down and black eyes,
Beaks yellow and pewter tipped, suddenly wafted with their nest (mom gone hunting),
End over end by a sudden storm wind-torn out of the crags and tumbling under
The sky's blue gullet-the rocks below coming up to meet them meet them meet them
And did a voice whisper in Hezekiah's ear saying:
Your children
Your children were the treasure
Did he say to himself: well, you never know how your kids will turn out.
I saw the backside of the Assyrian king Sennacherib
After he left 185,000 God-breathed dead in my land,
But *his* sons bashed in his skull while he was offering prayers
In the house of Nisroch, his god.

TOMATO PLANTS

In my head I am measuring stakes
For the two tomato plants
That are growing in the shade
Of the fig tree.
It has taken me a while
To become someone who is
Preoccupied with growing things
Whether I have planted them or not.
None of us can remember
Planting the tomato plants
They are an agricultural mystery
Not soon to be solved.
Perhaps it was the gardeners,
But I just don't know.
Here they are, under the fig tree,
And I feel responsible.
They have already produced
Clutches of small green fruit,
And the plant furthest along,
Is starting to bow itself to the planter brick.
All that matters is, unlike the onions,
Which I planted a while back,
And my second attempt at corn,
They are flourishing.
So, huzzah for the tomatoes,
The pumpkins (1/2) the red peppers,

The pink miniature rose bush
I planted for my wife.
The gardeners have a deal
With my next-door neighbor.
They collect their share of guavas
That grow on the side of the house.
Sometimes, it is like that:
The small, unlooked for gifts happen,
And you don't question God for them:
Whether it's a free sack of guavas,
Or a couple of tomato plants.

NESTS

The two abandoned wasp nests sit on my bedroom bureau,
Shaded the dingy, dirty gray of age-old candy wrappers.
I redeemed them both from the eaves outside my daughter's room
Quite a while back (to my wife's initial discomfort)
Courtesy of a couple deft and delicate jabs of a pool scoop.
Light as a jongleur's love, riddled with dozens of small round chambers,
Piled atop each other between small mounds of dry leaves and seashells,
Hedged in by the Peterson Field Guide to Birds of North America,
And the monthly bills, they lie amidst the glean of nature's lucre,
A little sad and forlorn without the frenzied loft and bustle
Of slender, angry black-yellow forms.
They offer a fine underline in theme next to the black turban snail shells,
With their weathered and faded spirals of dark blue and lavender
On their outer layer of calcite, with a splash of green iridescence
On the rim of the inner shell's mother-of-pearl.
I lean over the nests from time to time, wafting them across the bureau
With the imperceptible hiss of my breath, or lifting them to marvel
At God's ingenuity-the perfection of each small circular hole of ingress and
egress,
Picking them up as gently as if they were pieces of papyrus on loan from a
museum.
Outside the kitchen window on the long wooden sill,
By a small collection of driftwood daggers and sea stones: quartzite,
Conglomerate, schist, dolomite and granite,
Rest the equally small, fragile cups of two black towhee nests,
Made from bark, grass, a thin circle of blue-white trim for one

Dirty string and red ribbon for the other.
These I captured and redeemed from the high outside peak between the
Living room and my daughter's bedroom, upheld as they were by metal pipes.
I brought them down with the care with which a Japanese feudal Ashigaru
Would bring down a battle-routed samurai hiding in the heights of a spring
cedar.
I have had them for quite a while and they have sat there, unmolested
By the force of the elements and the vagaries of gardeners with blowers.
The inside whorls of dead grass and bark contain small bits of broken egg.
My daughter recently asked if she could pass them on to a friend
Who has a very keen interest in bird nests, and I agreed to give up one,
Just as long, I told her, as I was able to keep the other one for my collection.
When did I become so fascinated with abandoned nests and empty shells?
I can't say. I suppose I can say it's a cry from the unconscious
And one of those obvious metaphors that I tend to hate:
The reality that one day the kids will have to move on, leave the family domicile,
Strike out on their own, sans wings, stings, or sliding foot.
It's not even something more jejune and forgettable as
Intimations of mortality at sixty: the soul's egress from
Its cage of flesh-gliding with grace like a white-black albatross far away
From this life's fusty press court of shirts and skins.
No, it isn't the leaving of kids or leaving of life that leads me
To pile up wasp and black towhee nests, and brush the finger's pad
Over the calcium carbonate armor of blue and white of old mussel shells,
To hover over and contemplate them (occupant gone moved on)
And I am not even sure that I am just rediscovering nature and its
Amazements and miracles in old age (but there might be some of that).
I think
It
Is
Just
This:
With the end of the failed Rona madness mandates and awful lockdowns,
The end of two years of failed self-imprisonments, mishandling,
Mismanagement, small business closures and ma and pa vendor deaths,
I think

I am just darned glad to see that anyone or anything
Made it out of its
House.

STEGOSAURUS

"If I could only bring back one of these alive."
Carl Denham (in the 1933 King Kong)

I remember the sun-bedazzled days of running in circles in the backyard,
Then dropping to my back to clutch the grass, dizzied vision
Taking in the awesome cloud-pocked gullet of blue sky,
Thinking gravity would reverse itself and I would fly upwards
Lost forever from family and friends, the earth churning beneath me,
Bucking like a bronco or a whale with a half-dozen harpoons in its hide.
Nearby, in the grass, plastic dinosaurs and army men enacted their daily feud:
The Axis siding with Tyrannosaurus Rex, while the Allies, always,
Went with the underdog-Stegosaurus. To me, when I played with
My armies of saurians, soldiers and aliens, Stegosaurus was always
The Hero (with an assist from triceratops and ankylosaurus).
As a child, I had felt ineffable sorrow and anger when, in the original King Kong,
The filmmaker and jerk Carl Denham and his gun-packing crew
Had hammered the innocent lizard with shot and grenades,
(okay, he charged them, but these jokers could have taken another route
When steg wandered briefly out of their sight and firing range)
And after bringing him down, had spent that parting shot into the creature's
brainpan,
Denham's lot moving on as the dinosaur's spiked tail did its dying dance,
Like a punctured firehose or downed electrical cable.
As a child watching King Kong, I was always hit by the callousness
Of the last round expended into the thick skull of the prone creature,
Lying on its side and occasionally pawing the steamy air with a thick foot

(Two grenades had laid it out-there wouldn't be a third charge).
And I winced when-after the last shot-the soundtrack lent its emphatic note,
And the big head shot up, trembled, turning its unseeing eye on its killers before
It collapsed for good and all across the heated jungle humus
And I, felt pity for the dinosaur that got the first taste of contemporary ordnance,
The unfairness of it all-for a paradise breached by ugly-minded adventurers,
Interlopers out for a quick buck, dragooned by a goon with a map and mission.
I pitied the huge, ungainly being with its back a ridge of mini-Gibraltars,
Who was just cropping the green on Skull Island, puny brain dreaming limbic
dreams
Of fight or flight-whether Tyrannosaurus or Allosaurus was lurking somewhere
In the next patch of mangrove swamp, or behind the mighty arboreal giants
Wrapped in webs of shadow, creepers and liana vines,
But surely not expecting to be bombed and drilled with lead in the midst of his
Minor Late Jurassic musings on light's movement (something's movement)
Through the emperor ferns, light flaring from the wings of dragonflies
The size of mastiffs, light braising the wingtips of Skull Island's cranes and egrets
As they wove through the amplitude of tree-screen and sagging vines,
(but yes, there was light Light Light Light everywhere)
Shining like eider off a fur-patch of the great ape's shoulder as it moved
With the ease and elan of a gladiator through the great green that had never
known
Bomb, bullet, wiseacre repartee, only birdsong, bug buzz, tearing flesh and
snapping bone,
Or the distant throb and percussive counterpoint of tom-toms from the Great
Gate.
Did the spike-tailed lizard stop, lulled and comforted by the King's hoots and
burbling
As he passed-like a summer puff of cumulus cloud or a quick rain-shower?
Sometimes-as a kid-I imagined scenarios where Denham and his gang
Gave Stegosaurus a wide berth and the filmmaker, they waited for him to
Thud his way out of the narrow corridor of impending death,
And later, Denham being a bit more expansive and great of soul
After sending stun-bombed Kong into the Big Snooze for his voyage to New
York,
Saluted the spike-backed plant-eater with the Louisville slugger tail

From a comfortable distance and said, with the confidence of a carnival barker,
"Well, we'll be back for you on the next try and put you in the petting zoo.
I'll charge the kids 50 cents a ride. So, don't get too comfortable."
"Maybe we'll bring back one of those bird-things too-folks would pay a fortune
For a ride on one of those guys, huh, men?"
Imagined the shot not shot-the great tail that didn't writhe in slow-time
Emptying out the last bits of life in spasmodonic rise and fall.
That would have been the best scenario because there'd be no redo,
No second scow-chug to Skull Island to capture another wonder,
To pack some scale-hided leviathan in the cargo hold,
Simmered down with better knock-out bombs and chloroform.
No, there was no chance that Carl would be bankrolled another shot at fame,
Not after the total bankruptcy, public opprobrium and disgrace
Following the big ape's dive off the top of the Empire State Building.
No: Stegosaurus, Brontosaurus, Allosaurus, Elasmosaurus and Pteranodon
Wouldn't have to worry about another raid and capture run.
It would have been Denham stumbling through the streets of NYC,
Booze-soaked brain imagining endless treks through green hells of scale and hide,
Falling off broken rafts, upended tree bridges, the cliff-edge vine-rope
Being hauled up and up by a vast furry hand as living kites circled above and
below,
He'd awaken from nightmares of steaming jungle, teeth, earth lurching under
Unseen prehistoric impactors-screams of crew and creditors dogging him.
It would have ended in newspaper print for covers for the old huckster
As he caught his own prolonged Big Snooze on Central Park benches,
Flophouse beds, tenement alcoves, shop doorways,
Hawking copies of Skull Island's map as he begged for backers,
Until maybe someone related to one of Kong's victims,
Some traumatized ex-starlet, a vengeful mate off Captain Englehorn's ship,
Backed Denham up to the dead-end brick of a fog or rain-lashed alley,
And made him pay the bill for that voyage with blackjack, broken bottle, knife or
gun,
I never had a problem letting Stegosaurus win more than his share against
Tyrannosaurus Rex and his Axis allies.
I never had a problem breaking the rules to let him come back off the ropes
For a win.

RETURN TO PRAYER

Sometimes we have to reacquaint ourselves with the act of prayer:
We get out of the habit of a steady dialogue with God.
It happens: exhaustion and despondency bury us on a daily basis,
The words pulled down by the black abyssal tug of a wounded spirit's millstone,
Conscience and soul worn raw like a faded pair of Levis,
Sucked down like layers of dead plankton to the ocean floor
Our better thoughts and feelings weighed down by unreproved horrors
Abetted crimes and outrages marring the art of living,
The wall spackle of this world's evil and insane incantations
Working its vile sorcery on the day's allowance of faith, grace and love.
The soul becomes less able, and we forget The Lamb of Life,
The simple balm of the gospel-our allowance of parables and beatitudes,
The broken bread and the love that made the long trek to Golgotha,
Bearing the cross for our sake-we forget it all for a while,
And these dragon days continue to take their awful and relentless toll,
The conversation with God dialed down to the sporadic rain-sizzle
Of a fighter pilot's radio-chatter pouring from shattered cockpit,
Smoking plane rammed between jungle giants, wrapped in lianas.
The return to communication can be as easy and simple as
The realization you haven't given your wife a kiss in months,
So, standing in the kitchen limned by the heavy particulate light
Of sunset's magical transition from rose and gold to twilight's blue and cinder,
Waiting for her to pass again between counter and table,
You slip your arm around her waist and place one on the corner of her lips,
Surprising a wry smile from her-and it all comes back,
The evening's precious bouquet of honeysuckle, rose and jasmine,

The words and need remembered, praise recalled,
Soul making the sandal-trek, not a staff, scrip or money bag in sight,
But heading out again-purpose recovered, God-time recovered:
Much like pulling up to an oft rented vacation cabin,
Taking in the in the half-remembered scintillance of creek shine
Behind the vaulting green of sycamore and elm,
Jay song/dove tabor/owl hoot, healing smell of woodsmoke,
And frustration and weariness fly like listening to an old engine tick down.
Other times, it isn't half that easy: even when you find the time again,
You struggle to find the right words, the right things to ask for,
The feather-soft ease of unburdening that had come so easy before,
But now, is as difficult as paring an armored artichoke down to its heart,
Past the extraneous leaves and poisoned frizz green as a dryad's hair.
Sometimes, it is like you're by yourself sitting at a party in your home,
And someone, maybe it is your wife or an the in-laws haul out
The ancient videos of your kids as toddlers tearing through Christmas paper,
Clapping a gift box to their hairless head, pulling on a stuffed horse's mane,
And just then-as imperceptible as a midnight snowfall,
The shadow passes-it impinges, crossing the living room floor,
And the estranged father (or mother) you haven't spoken to in years,
Whom you invited out of a half-felt/half-sincere magnanimity
Lowers themselves on the other end of the couch you picked,
And not turning your head to look, you mark the sag and groan of upholstery
And the squeal of tired and taxed springs years old and
Seconds bleed into minutes-the rest of the room's chatter phased out
And finally he (or she) says, "Well, they grow up fast, don't they?"
And you nod and hem and fiddle with your glass or a ceramic paperweight
And eventually, after making several attempts to frame them
The words come.

STUDENT LOAN FORGIVENESS

One grows bone-weary of such unmitigated stupidity,
Like an old state trooper standing at the edge of a broken guardrail,
Mountain road and midnight's snowfall at his back,
Shaking his head, having seen this time and again,
Turning away in disgust from the chimney plume of wreck smoke,
Boiling up from below to join the cold involution of drifting flakes,
Lowering his flashlight as he adjusts his body-cam,
Recording, amidst the jittery blue and red roll
Of his cruiser's visibar lights,
Clearly visible amidst the snow and glass scatter
In front of the rail:

The beer-soaked bits
Of dashboard madonnas.

HARMONIES

Coming to a stop at the corner light
Returning from my daughter Victoria's
Morning violin lesson
I cast a glance at my child
Sitting in the backseat on the passenger side
Headphones on, eyes closed
Cradling her violin case in her lap
Nodding her head lost in the harmonies
The peaceful notes, chords and noodling
Of another sun-shot early Saturday afternoon
And I smile because my child is happy
And I am happy for her
And music sweet as summer cider
Hale and healthy as August's buttery air
Fair as the brass clasp of a gusty gazebo band
Fills my heart surprises a smile from me
A smile that becomes an outright grin
Which dies with the whiplash of obscenity
The young homeless man
Stripped to the waist his t-shirt balled up in his hand
Raving as he stalks angrily down the sidewalk
Minotaur tremens rippling through hard muscle
Faded tattoos writhing across sun-bronzed biceps
Jerking his head, screaming unintelligible threats
Through his filthy beard at no one at hand
Before stopping to aim a vicious kick at the air

I roll up the windows and hit the automatic lock
Chill of autumn leaves at my neck
Waiting for the light to change
Waiting for the man and his squalid program
To move on

FATHERS/SENNACHERIB.

Isaiah 37:36-38
English Standard Version
[36] And the angel of the Lord went out and struck down 185,000 in the camp of
the Assyrians.
And when people arose early in the morning, behold, these were all dead
bodies. [37] Then Sennacherib king of Assyria departed and returned home and
lived at Nineveh. [38] And as he was worshiping in the house of Nisroch his god,
Adrammelech and Sharezer, his sons, struck him down with the sword. And
after they escaped into the land of Ararat, Esarhaddon his son reigned in his
place.

Well, there's no good face to put on this one, mighty Nisroch of the eagle's wings!
I don't care what the priests, scribes, soothsayers and eunuchs say:
You raise a siege after waking up to 185,000 Sons of Ashur dead
Swords sheathed, spears racked, corselets unmarred and blazing like siege fires,
And the truth is you lose half your authority by the time you chariot out of there!
I impaled the last priest who said if you win scores and lose one, have you really
lost?
Yes, you've lost! That damned Hezekiah and his Hebrew rabble are there now,
Laughing their asses off, claiming their God death-breathed the whole lot of
those troops!
Ha! I saw the bodies: the black swellings-and the mice, the mice eating shield rims
And bow-cases-but what kind of plague comes on a camp in one night?
(the eyes all those eyes open and dawn sheen souls roaring into the air loud as the
Euphrates)
How am I to commemorate this one, Nisroch of the raptor's beak?

I can say I reduced the other cities, and I surrounded Jerusalem, I caged them
Like mangy hill bears-I penned them up like gazelles-but penned up isn't dead
and defeated!
I just don't see how we're going to write this one up and sell it to the home folks.
It's not like when we smashed those stubborn Elamites and uppity snobs at
Babylon:
No mounds of slain, no prisoners with hooks in the nose stumbling behind the
chariots,
No files of prisoners as multitudinous as the pismires of the earth!
I need to retrench and flay and decapitate a few of the most likely nobles to
revolt,
I need to look at the numbers and the likelihood of new levies for a second strike,
I'll sack the subjected provinces for the cream of the crop of their soldiery and I'll
return!
By Nisroch and Ashur I will see Hezekiah dragged away with a hook in his nose,
I'll make a memorial of the lopped limbs of his troops and peel their skin like
cucumbers!
How did this happen: did I not wear the medallions of Nisroch and Ashur to
protect me
From the attacks of the evil god Ilu Limnu and the medallion of winged Pazuzu
To protect me from the attacks of the demon Labartu and that of Lilu
To protect me from the attacks of Shedim-were these not about my neck
When I fastened on sword, bolstered my spear and slung my bow when I rode to
the foe?
185,000 dead! There's just no way to put a good face on this!
But who can't come back from such a thing, it is not impossible, is it, Nisroch?
Poems/French 62.
I turned Babylon into a dung-heap: I killed their best and hauled the rest into
slavery,
I smashed every wall, toppled every stone, sowed the earth with salt and planted
nettles.
Who says I cannot come back from this and make a second go at the Hebrews?
Who says I cannot take Jerusalem from Hezekiah-sometimes a reversal is
fortunate,
But how do I put a good face on this-185,000 dead without a blow struck
(they looked like they were sleeping ready for the trumpet rouse how could this be)

I have taken lions with the bow who is this Hezekiah I have taken lions with the bow,

It is a thing to be reversed-I will surround his turtledove with hawks then see how he sings!

Nisorch and Ashur will grow me new armies do I not wear medallions against the demons,

Have I no confidence in corslet of copper scale, spear, sword and arrow,

Have I not strong sons, a brace of young lions at my right and left hand?

By the beak of great Nisroch, I will make surround Nineveh with the Hebrews' heads,

I will haul Hezekiah out of that nest of resistors like a fish, take his eyes, then impale him,

I will impale him on the highest stake hewn and that will be the end of them,

Have I not a brace of young lions, a nest of eagle chicks to stand at my side

While I fire the first arrow into Jerusalem-my brave and valiant boys,

Champing like stallions at the bridle-war-steeds whose hooves split helms,

Am I not blessed with heirs who will not hesitate to wade into the torrents of panic,

Spirited youths, crowned with glory, who will be as high dunes between me and the host,

When a father suffers a reversal, should he not turn to the son of the right and left hands?

But how do you put a good face on this-185,000 dead without a blow struck,

How still they looked under the shadow-coil of the vultures,

Dead without a blow struck-in one night-this is not a thing that can be done,

But I will return with my boys Arda-Mullisu and Essrhaddon

With the princes of my flesh blood might I will return and make an end of them

And the memorials I will build I will build Nisroch a new temple

Do I not wear the medallions of Pazuzu and Lilu to protect me from the demons

Ilu Limnu and Labartu am I not king of this great kingdom Assyria

This cradle ant-hill of soldiers sons of Ashur and Nisroch washed in blood's charm

(185,000 dead how do I put a good face on this how do I put a good face on it)

With the princes of my old age I will

Sons sons what what why do you draw why do you draw

This is the house of Nisroch

I am yours and you are mine you are my boys

You do not dare you do not draw sword sword sword!

ALMOST AUTUMN

October's hot Santa Anas notwithstanding we are almost there:
The short days of generous lead-bellied clouds and wind-spun leaves,
Morning skies the hue of gunmetal gulls, bobolink or catbird,
The late day lattices of thick, roseate light, ingot-bright sunset bleeds
Between the season-scraped limbs, branches and boughs
Of elm, oak, sycamore and pine: brief days, long nights;
Summer's lease is nearly done, and you aren't sorry for that.
It's time to trade out lemonade for hot tea and pumpkin spice lattes,
Daydreaming at the breakfast table as you watch the sharp light
Helix off the undersides of the green-reddish leaves
Of the clutch of prunus trees over-hanging the back wall,
While a dirty brown-gray squirrel undulates down the brickwork
Like a target in a carnival shooting-gallery and you smile
Over your coffee-cup and think, the local tuxedo cat
Is missing out on the big win. Sharp light and sharp thoughts,
That's how the mornings start and even birdsong seems
Filed down to a good flensing or clamming knife.
And the dying season sidles up to you with the calculating aplomb
Of a cold beauty who plants a cider-sweet kiss on your lips
Leaving a fall of chaff-dandruff in your hair before she's off,
Nothing at all like summer's heat-beat maid of torpor and heliotrope dreams.
Here are the days of cold gusts doing glissandos across the fur
Of your neighbors' greyhound or American bully,
Like a pianist warming the keys up for a recital.
The sweaters and scarves hauled out like malefactors given parole,
The watch caps, ski masks, hoodies and sweatshirts following suit,

Hands seek pockets, fingers smooth down wind-flipped collars,
Blankets and comforters liberated from closets and bins.
Cold, cold-she's never warm enough and you find yourself pacing
Between bedroom and kitchen, taking inventory of Stuff: in the house,
And out in the garage-never quite committing to take it out to the curb,
But marking the shelves-finding a sack of old photos squirreled
Away between sleeping-bags, wondering how they got out there.
The dying season has you ruminating on Old Stuff,
Like being the last guy in a bar at Closing Time,
Listening to a fat man with a sax blow the soul-scape notes
Telling you he is sure as hell hungry.
This is how it works as the temperature drop and you transition
To crow-time, grackle-time: everyone has season discontents,
And they are not shy about voicing them, either.
Arguments and train of thoughts start and stop like the hop
And dire doll-shine gaze of crow murder staking out
The dry, brittle patches of your lawn or front gutter.
You nearly butt hips or elbows because the house is too small,
The two of you two like Jupiter and Venus on a planetary conjunction,
As you both make your bids for the thermostat,
Or the teapot when it's in mid-squeal like a midnight freight engine's whistle.
More and more, the brief late-night trips out to the back patio occur,
And as the moon-striped leaves talk their parchment husk lingo,
And the branches whicker and etch constellation signs in the
Night's diamond-dusted skin, you let nightbird and wind weft lull you,
And-half-superstitiously-look for a contrail of dying green,
Mind back-flipping like an old frog into a silty pond of mortal intimations,
Before cricket chirrup and bone-whittling cold, send you back inside,
And you quell the memory of the morning, day or evening dust ups
With a hug, an encircling arm or a long kiss,
And the two of you make-up with the avidity of a barn-loft roll,
The balm of a burnt-orange harvest moon on your skins,
The jamb of fiddle-sizzle in your blood and hers,
Stretch of muscle and tendon like a bow string,
And you smile down at her as you forget the chill,
The leaf-dribble on the roof and scrape of branches under the eaves,
And all you can see all she can see all that can be is
The windfall ruckus of apple orchard in her eyes and yours.

AUTUMN WOODSMOKE

Woodsmoke is a lanyard that takes you by the wrist,
Like a bluetick coon dog or brash beagle pulling you down country roads
Seeded with sunset's last toss of red and amber welding sparks,
Fields of glassine wheat one side, apple and pear orchard on the other.
That's how you feel when out of sorts in the eve, restless and achy,
An unconscious need for an ergonomic chair made of
Moss-corseted tree stump or creek stone calling you from the couch folds,
Making you step out of the house for a quick gander of starlight,
The night sky an upended robber's bag of interrupted gem theft,
Strewn by masked miscreants in preacher's suits waving snub-nosed revolvers,
Dumping the bag and heading for the back way
Because the cops showed up early to this dance and thieves don't tango.
But what was I saying I was saying is that woodsmoke,
Stops you in your tracks and says autumn is here friend,
Its night-whisked whorls are as much a transition as the calendar's page,
Summer's lingering heat cut with breeze fumble and blade-sharp light,
It is a sure announcement that the days of braise are done.
And the dying season with its celebrations and caveats has come 'round.
Smell that-mark the waft of chimney's white plume few houses down,
And though you are just a city-suburb guy or gal at heart,
You loiter on the cement walk, taking in kindling's sky-smear
Drifting up in sinuous dance to kiss Andromeda or Perseus,
Feeling tension's release accompanied by bird blather and cricket chirp.
The swift slap of a walker's sneakers on the sidewalk,
The swift flare of a bike light crossing the street's entrance,
The plaintive cries of puppies near the end of the cul-de-sac;

That is when it hits you: *where did summer go and why did I do so little?*
Then, shaken, you turn your head and take time to gawk
At moon-fire refulgent as a fog-horn's candle on the Oregon coast,
Coming off the roof of your neighbor's new Jayco or Sequoia Salt RV,
And you almost expect to hear a mandolin's chord override the chill sibilance
Of leaf and limb-air's arresting filigree for harvest, hayrick and bonfire,
And as you watch more smoke pour from your neighbor's roof,
Without thinking, you raise your hand from your side and open it:
Expecting moon's glint on a fistful of shelled walnuts.

EXHAUSTED

So done you wish you could drift like a stringer of trout.

FATHERS/RUSSIAN PRESIDENT VLADIMIR PUTIN

"As he wages war in Ukraine, Russian President Vladimir Putin will be welcoming a baby girl with his ex-gymnast lover — and is grumbling that he already has enough daughters, according to a report." (New York Post Story)
Psalm 127:3-4
English Standard Version
[3] Behold, children are a heritage from the Lord,
the fruit of the womb a reward.
[4] Like arrows in the hand of a warrior
are the children[a] of one›s youth.
If we were inhuman (if we were inhuman) we would be tempted

To raise the lip in the sickle of derision, in a smile of absolute cynicism,
Were we standing in the remains of a hospital nursery or NICU,
Shattered bits of incubators, charred streamers of blankets and bandages,
Half-deflated, stone and glass-dusted Birthday balloons,
Jelly-fishing up out the concrete and pipe fringed eye of ceiling caused
By the missiles unleashed by an Mi-24 helicopter gunship,
Or turned into a momentary snow-globe of swirling debris
By the lightning-quick pass of a pair of Russian "Frogfoot" jet fighters.
If we were not human, we would reflect upon your recent grousing
That your gymnast lover Alina was gifting you with another daughter
Rather than the son you had hoped for, and we would release
A belly-buster of sick and mordant laughter-the kind that comes up
Like the bile of a bad meal while you breath in black anaconda/mamba coils
Of burial pit smoke, watching them go up to be whipped into boas

By the passage of air's screaming armor and thudding rotors,

Feeding the bleak overhang of ash-blanched sky.

We would, if we were standing there in the invaded lands,

Consider the happenstance of seed and misdeed, birth and death,

Of the God that knits us all in the womb even in the midst of catastrophe,

Whether our parents wanted us or not: for children are a blessing,

A heritage from the lord-even to dictators, tyrants and destroyers.

Did The Father make Herod's wife barren even when he sought

To slay the Holy Lamb and Author of Eternal Life?

It is a shame that you have enough daughters, surely it is a shame!

If we were inhuman (if we were inhuman) we would be tempted

To clap a hand over our mouths and give way to non-stop giggles

As we stood in a child's room, their home cross-section by tank shells,

Like a doll's house upended into chaos by a malicious hand,

Listening to and looking at the crayon-colored pictures flapping

On the walls-half held by tape as others sail out the ragged aperture,

Taken into the factory/foundry fume of a cratered street's bulge of smoke and fire,

The crudely drawn boy holding the smiling dog with the too long tongue,

The little girl hugging a friend on a green hill surrounded by

Sunflowers large as date palms etched in yolk yellow and burnt brown,

We would mark the certificates of achievement, the photos of

Daughter and Dad, Daughter and Mother, Son and All

(does it really make a difference in the order of oblivion)

(does it really make a difference in the melting of flesh)

(in the atomization and ash-heap of bone)

The photo of the family summer vacation to Tylihul Estuary,

Or Arena Lviv, Lviv national Art Gallery, or maybe just

The proud parents standing next to the daughter in graduation robes,

Holding up her diploma to whomever it was that took the shot.

Do we not remember someone's daughter, earlier this year,

Dressed in formal red gown, eyes old but determined, going through

Her graduation ceremony in the ruins of her school?

We have seen these things as sleepers wakened by a lost dog's bay from an ice crevasse,

We have seen these things-things unshelled like wyverns and cockatrices

Stirring and fanning their wings in the morning's blameless Bengal light.

Would we not stand there, listening to far-off arms fire as the wind keens,

And ask how a child's life could come to this?

It is a shame that you have enough daughters, surely it is a shame!

Because we are human (and we/and you are human) we might sidle up to you,

Still choking on our uncontrollable gales of damnable hilarity,

We might find it in our self-will to tolerate the share of molecules,

The stump-water smell of seared conscience and unreason,

And ask you questions, Mr. President, regarding the vagaries of Family Planning

Versus families introduced to the unwanted egress of wanted children

Translated, wafted out of play, wonder, mirth, sunlight, love and life life life,

By the swift pass of war's dragons or trundle and cannon of tank and carrier

Into blotches, smears and Rorschachs of blood and wall-gristle,

Smoking bone scrabble-we would speak to you of such things,

As to how-how you could bemoan the upcoming arrival of a baby-girl,

Without human reflection, nuance, understanding and self-irony,

When you have taken so many from their parents,

Deprived grandparents of granddaughters and grandsons,

Filled broken hearts with a generation of ghosts,

Buzzing and battering memories like moths wrapping the fool's gold

Of wing-dust around a dusty kitchen bulb.

How many young ones-left bereft-are doing whatever they can,

For the next cup of sour water, the next dirty chunk of bread,

Crouching in a dark apartment house or rocket-leveled church,

Doing whatever they need to stay warm?

It is a shame that you have enough daughters, surely it is a shame!

Because we are human (we are not nonhuman/neither are you) we might ask

Whether your heart will soften when your lover the gymnast Alina

Shows you the burbling girl-child rowing her limbs in her cradle,

Or sleeping soundly on her side-thumb in her mouth, arm wrapped

Around a stuffed animal or the figure of Nikita The Tanner, the knight who

Saved the children of Kiev from the triple-headed dragon Zmey Gorynych,

But only after Prince Vladimir of Kiev had hundreds of kids surround the house

Of that noble did he break down (if only you were that Vladimir!).

When you see your new baby will you relent (or will it happen on Smart Phone),

And find yourself humming Sleeping Tired Toys to her unconsciously, or

A Cricket Sings Behind The Stove-will you show the lineaments of adoration,

Or frown because God has not bestowed a little *bogatyr* on you?

Will you resign and say, well, Mariya and Yekatarina will have a tiny sister,

And who knows what the future holds-there may yet be a boy,

If you are victorious will there not be time for the making of a son?

But now, when you look upon the sleeping form or wonder-filled eyes of the babe,

Will you see the daughters of Kyiv in her face and remember

The salvation offered by the child in the manger to His children,

If they repent and believe on him-will you have mercy on the children

Of the Ukraine to whom you have become a Zmey or a Zilant?

Will you think upon the Christ child-the little prince without a crown,

And remember mercy-remember compassion?

It is a shame that you have enough daughters, surely it is a shame!

IMPECUNIOUS

I wanted to use the word impecunious in a poem,
But it just wasn't working out (I had hit a block),
So, I turned to my cryptid friends to help me out,
To provide an example of the adjective meaning:
To have little or no money.
The Oklahoma Octopus, a freshwater Cephalopod
Living in the depths of Lake Thunderbird whipped a huge tentacle
Orange as a Mandarin's silk gown in curt refusal and scooted back
Under a big rock: he was planning a drowning,
And, shy and sensitive, couldn't be bothered with such bluster.
So, I turned to Bigfoot for this one and he stepped
Out of the preternatural darkness of Sequoia National Forest, CA,
The westering light setting patches of his shaggy reddish-brown fur afire,
While he swatted at deerflies with a padded hand big as a catcher's mitt.
I had not written a poem about his true whereabouts-or spilled the beans
To any number of angry "forest wives" seeking back alimony.
He would send me a grateful email each autumn.
He posed next to one of the arboreal giants, yellowish tusks
Jutting from a nervous primate's smile, and he said,
In his voice which was a half-growl, half-buzz full of ape glottal,
"Okay, you've got about thirty seconds of my time,"
"And then I'm going to go back to my cave and listen to
Some Ben Folds."
"Impecunious," he whoofed, sending a family of deer
Hightailing it back into the overgrowth, surprising a
Shrill scream out of a red-tailed hawk, and scattering

A bunch of Carolina chickadees. "If you spend your life
Trying to find me, you are likely to wind up impecunious."
And with that, singing "The Ascent of Stan" to himself,
He turned and ambled back into the over-awing green and sun-sprinkle
Glad to have done me a solid with the muse.
But after a couple minutes he crunched his way back to
Where I was sitting on a rock scribbling away in my notebook,
And clearing his throat, spoke in his avalanche-tumble tone:
"However, if Scarlet Johannson or Emilia Clarke were to assay the task
Of tracking me down, I might be prevailed upon to leave an obvious trail."
And then, launching into "The Sound of The Life of The Mind,"
He chuffed and burbled his way back to his woodland fane,
Dirty shafts of imperial red and bronze light breaking across his back,
The Stellar jays, chickadees and yellowthroats returning to their tunes.

THE BOUNTY OF GOD

This morning, the bounty of God was a small orange tomato,
Plucked from one of the two plants growing beneath the fig tree,
Unaffected by sunscald, fruit cracks or blossom end rot.
It wound up part of my morning's breakfast just as another
Had garnished yesterday's lunch, along with a solitary not-too sweet fig.
The tomato plant was someone's anonymous gift, I don't know who:
Neither I nor anyone else in my family can recall planting it.
I accept it with gratitude as I do the Tiger Swallowtail's brief flounce
Over the back wall, or the day songs of finch, towhee and sparrow,
The sly slouch of a beloved tuxedo cat across dividing brick,
Tail switching-chatoyant pupils widening when we catch him in action.
A tiny green grasshopper, barely more than half of my knuckle,
Sat poised on a nearby leaf, legs tented, refusing to launch itself
Into the void or chance a landing-pad recovery on another leaf.
He stood his ground like a solitary museum guard
Cowering behind a drape in the dark early morn, watching bad men
In black clothes and balaclavas cut the glass over a papyrus or gem case:
Too scared to make the right call, and too loyal to leave the premises.
I do my best not to startle the little guy-live and let live.
I find it hard to kill the pests when they are juveniles.
His new green glister and smallness-shorn of armor-touches me.
The bounty of God is still bounty even if it arrives in increments.
In drips and drabs as when a hummingbird feeder is down to
The last few ounces of syrup-but the grateful bird blurring in place
Is happy enough that morning's brindle provides a few drops:
A single spring for Ishmael or a quick drink for a bird-it's all good.

The bee sleeping in the depths of the red hibiscus would agree, I am sure.
And all things considered, I have to admit the same.
I am grateful to God for a few tomatoes from a plant I didn't plant,
A few figs from our finnicky tree's summer crop.
I hope I can coax more from the earth by this next year, but
I am content with the undeserved loving kindnesses I have received.
The few struggling corn seedlings in a corner of the backyard,
The weathered black-brown crow decoy hanging nearby
Like a spurned pinata full of nothing but hard aniseed twists
Remind me that the bounty of God has its limits but also instructs:
It reminds us as amateur growers-Old Adams with our spade,
That we're not in Paradise but always East of Eden,
Learning the dirt-smeared lexicon of the Land of Nod,
Reacquainting ourselves with the footprints barely impressed
In Eden's feathery grass to the cracked loam warmed by angel sword.
The garden jargon that never came up before The Fall:
Seed, mulch, row, cordon, slips, bulbs-all of it, fulfilling or frustrating,
The satisfaction of seeing something nurtured from hard ground,
There is something about it that I, an amateur, cannot explain.
As I place the tomato on my plate, sipping my coffee, reading Luke 14,
About the healing of a man on the sabbath (how He finessed the lawyers!),
I thank God for the bounty that is more than just food.
I thank Him for His Word that can still be read in this country
Glad that it hasn't been banned here as it has in totalitarian countries,
The lands of Islam, in North Korea, in China or the "stan" nations,
"offending" parts excised by the government-as Canada has done.
The aeration, irrigation, rotation, direct sow and pollination continue,
And the yield: a bumper crop, a full, fridge crisper or spud bin,
The bounty of God goes on-wisdom and faith breaking through
Earth's kind/unkind crust-green hopes feeling for the sun
Just as we are feeling our way to The Son through belief and hard study,
Removing the doubts that The Enemy sows as we would an invasive weed,
Or bean aphids, Japanese beetles, leafhoppers, squash bugs and weevils.
This morning the bounty of God was a small orange tomato,
Barely more than a couple of bites-joy of soft skin and juice,
As well as a solid reading from the Book of Luke with a garnish of psalms
Along with some of the victories won by King David in 2 Samuel.
It is enough in this world, I assent. It is enough in this world.

THE MAN IN THE BLOOD RED LIGHT

"We must end this uncivil war that pits red against blue, rural versus urban,
conservative versus liberal. We can do this if we open our souls instead of
hardening our hearts."
From President Joe Biden's Inaugural Address 01/20/21
"What we're seeing now is the beginning or the death knell of an extreme
MAGA philosophy. It's not just Trump, it's the entire philosophy that underpins
the — I'm going to say something, it's like semi-fascism."
From President Joe Biden's Speech to The Nation 09/01/22

I liked you best and pitied you well when you were The Ghost-Greeter:
Lost and wandering away from the podium with your hand outstretched,
To glad-hand (???) Nebo/Baal/Marduk/Xipe Toltec/Nisroch/Lucifer/Asmodeus/
Pazuzu,
I don't know who-or if you just wanted someone-anyone-to lead you by the hand
Away from this ghastly, unlovely gig you have created-someone to remove you
from shame,
From questions it was never in you to answer-as if you were allowed to answer
them,
From the terrible consequences of your destructive, fatal decisions,
Someone from somewhere-anywhere-moved by pity/compassion/mercy
To whisk you away from the reality of misrule's disaster and confusion:
Like a cop pulling rottweilers out of the dog-pit's sawdust and blood,
Someone making a saving of gaming-cocks before the heel-spurs collide,
The Coup de gras for the stumbling bull spined by the picadors' lances,
Lurching for the matador's crimson (you saw red) muleta, barely able to raise its
horns.

For those moments I forgot the open borders, inflation, high pump prices,

The mutilators of children-this nation's adulated surgeons of Cybele.

When you were The Ghost-Greeter, the Glad-Hander of Shadows,

The injunctions of God to pray for those in positions of power and authority,

Was possible in those moments-when you shuffled off like a St. Anthony swine.

But when you stood in the lurid glare as red as a blood moon's baneful claret,

Hectoring, shaking your fists-excoriating half the nation you had pledged to lead,

Dementia's dybbuk operating from your own script-I reflected on the Apostle Peter's words,

And how we were to keep them close to our hearts in these Post-Christian/Pre-Antichrist times:

To be subject for the Lord's sake to every human institution-emperors or governors.

And I remembered the Apostle Paul's reminder in Romans 13 that rulers,

Be they Nero, Trajan or Diocletian-were not a terror to good works,

But ordained by God-put into power by God and that weighed on my heart.

The words of John Calvin, that when God judges a nation, He gives them wicked rulers

Also scrabbled at my ruminations like wind-stirred elm branches across roof tiles.

And I asked myself, struggling as one does with the daily quicksilver shifts

Between summer's fading braise and autumn's slow, cool sidle,

Poems/French 75.

Cold fronts and warm fronts producing mid-latitude cyclones,

I replayed Peter and Paul's words in my mind and wondered: is that still true today?

I winced and wondered at words that lead in their way to concertina wire and camps,

To the truncheons and guns of fat beer and onion-breathed guards,

To cones of lights and the leash-strain of brutal dogs with bared fangs,

Literal, or just ideas sown in the fallow fields of an impoverished intellect.

(had he forgotten the Summer of Love 2020-had he forgotten CHAZ)

I considered the slow death of a nation through exhortations of separation and division,

The shift of tribal tent canvas and peg from another's across snow pile and crow tree,

The distance of barely flaring campfires in the long winter dark.

The words of King Rehoboth fated to divide ancient Israel into south and north
Impinged (my father chastised you with whips, but I will chastise you with
scorpions),
And once divided, Samaria's fall to the Assyrians and Judah's to the Babylonians.
And here was the reply of Christ to those who said He had a demon even as He
cast out
Demons from their sons and daughters-if Satan casts himself out can his
kingdom stand?
Can any kingdom or nation divided against itself stand?
(there are things that must be gotten away and shaken they must be shaken)
(the things that shall not be shaken will stand the things that must stand will
stand)
I looked at the demented man in the blood red light playing the part he could
never fill,
The Mario Bava Italian giallo gell of scarlet on the eagle and its arrows,
The stiffly posed marines resembling Palpatine's red guards with their force pikes,
(the moment you spoke you were fated to become a meme for weeks)
And I despaired at the utter crudity of such things as much as what they
portended.
As the Ghost-Greeter, I liked you best and pitied you well,
Lost and wandering away from the podium with your hand outstretched,
To glad-hand (???) Nebo/Baal/Marduk/Xipe Toltec/Nisroch/Lucifer/Asmodeus/
Pazuzu:
To whom did you stretch your hand-who did you see who would take your hand?
In a quiet voice, ruminations caught between waxing and waning moons,
I asked the Apostle Paul about the opposite of his words in Romans 13:
And what of rulers who become a terror to good works?
But he did not answer me.

IDENTIFIED

There was once a trans-species man who identified as a deer.
There was once a quartet of gentlemen who identified as hunters.
They Fudd-plugged his delusion with hot lead on a spring afternoon,
Hitting him twice in the haunch, sending him screaming to the ground,
Where he pawed the air with his hoof prosthetics and slammed his customized antlers
Into the sun and shadow-dappled earth, bleeding out beneath
The towering blue Douglas firs and wind-rifled pines while his assailants,
Coming out of their camo-colored blind at the edge of the field,
Ashen-faced and clutching their Marlin 366s and Weatherby Vanguards,
Wondered *what the hell this nut was thinking* dressing up
In Brooks Brothers Buck and Rut wear and crossing their line of fire,
And whether they could work up a decent Wendigo Defense
To mitigate the crime of mistakenly nailing a six-foot tall bipedal elk.
Maybe one of their number pointed out that Wendigos wended
Around Quebec and Ontario and as far as Minnesota but they were nowhere near
Those locales and that they had to face the fact they were simply screwed,
The dude in the deerskin *was a dude* and they were in a world of hurt.
I have no idea if they made the call to the ranger station to bring in
An ambulance chopper, or made a deal with a jaundice-eyed wolf pack to
Dispose of the evidence-but let's figure the better angels of their nature kicked in
As the man moaned about his leg and yelled about the gross victimization of the
Small but dedicated trans-species community, eyes rolling up white
As he went in and out of shock like a pod of dolphins
Through scintillant sets of emerald-colored waves and swells.

But let's assume

They did

The Right Thing

No appeal to wolves, bears or bobcats to roll up to make the save

Deer Man's gambol in the Arcadian green was done and they were not

Bringing any venison home for the larder-at least none the wife would touch.

Maybe they all looked at one another uneasily from beneath their cap brims,

And in a sort of dawning, horrified gestalt assisted by the spicy metallic scent of blood

And spoor fog of panic and culpability that there could be a petite lady

Waiting nearby or in another part of the forest, posing as a doe expecting her beau,

Who might have heard the shot and was already leaping and bounding back to her auto

To break out a Ruger for some payback.

Even worse: maybe there were infinite numbers of *identifying* bears, boars,

Horses, badgers, weasels, rabbits hurrying over armed with fatal facsimiles of

Fangs, hooves, trotters and all-maybe the whole forest was absolutely *insane*

And didn't identify *as a forest*

The brooks as brooks

The streams as streams

(where would it end)

(where does it end)

Me, if I had to identify as other, my ambition would be much simpler:

I would just like to identify as *well-travelled.*

Given the state of the economy and current life imperatives, this is a delusion

No less severe than those passing themselves off as cats, dogs, deer,

Golden dragon-kind, non-binary Monarch butterflies or office blocks.

SANTORINI

There are times, when soul weary, I would say to my God:
I would give anything to find myself walking hand in hand with my wife,
Down a narrow street in Santorini, Greece, our ears riffled by zither and lute,
Blinding house block white as cowry shells pressing in,
Salmon-scaled clouds and blue sky overhead,
Yellow-legged gulls and Cory's Shearwater bobbing on the thermals,
Explosions of fuchsia purple and red bougainvillea,
Detonations of blossom and bloom dark as blood,
Going off on terraces, in garden plots, from roof tiles as
One end of the street quails before the soul-lofting scintillance
Of the Aegean's vast blue-green swells, and the other,
The heat-hazed outline of robin blue church dome.
In lieu of the indescribable beauties of Your kingdom Lord
I would be content with such sights.

FEET

John 13:5-11
English Standard Version
5 Then he poured water into a basin and began to wash the disciples' feet and to wipe them with the towel that was wrapped around him. 6 He came to Simon Peter, who said to him, "Lord, do you wash my feet?" 7 Jesus answered him, "What I am doing you do not understand now, but afterward you will understand." 8 Peter said to him, "You shall never wash my feet." Jesus answered him, "If I do not wash you, you have no share with me." 9 Simon Peter said to him, "Lord, not my feet only but also my hands and my head!" 10 Jesus said to him, "The one who has bathed does not need to wash, except for his feet,[a] but is completely clean. And you[b] are clean, but not every one of you." 11 For he knew who was to betray him; that was why he said, "Not all of you are clean."

The Son of Man did not wash Judas' feet:
The traitor left the Left Supper before the Lord could wash his feet
Along with the rest of The Twelve.

Was it a mercy?
Was it a mercy?
What sorrow, what weary grief the Son of Man would have felt,
Had he applied the basin's cool water to the well-worn feet of Judas Iscariot,
Watching the day's dirt and dust sloughing away from the sole but not the soul,
The feet that would push on-guard dogged to Gethsemane's Garden,
Powering of betrayal's swift locomotion of skin/muscle/bone,
Arches, ankles, toes, heels-marking the creases and calluses,
The tanned overlay of phalange and tarsal, the flow of muscle and tendon,

The healing cuts-He would recall times when they had borne their owner
With him and the others down one dusty road to another as they shared The
Truth,
From miracle-starved hamlets to parable-puzzling crowds,
To the confrontations with the scheming Pharisees and scribes,
To the sick room in Nain where He raised the widow's son,
To The Sermon on The Mount, to the Feeding of The Five Thousand.
He knew every inch of them-they were a reality before they were knitted
In the womb, crossed under the fetus' buttocks-before the babe Judas
Took his first unsteady steps across the home floor,
Smiling at the outstretched arms of his parents, stumbling, falling,
Pushing himself up off the floor to try again and again,
Getting over hurt and spill of tears to make the child's journey
From floor crawl to standing standing like mother and father,
And later, carrying him from the root-weave of skepticism
About his ankles to the light, free step of conviction and faith?
How many miles had those feet wended, abraded by rock and thistle,
Skinned by grit caught between skin and worn sandal's cushion,
Caked with sea-sand and shell-bits when they had to board the boat,
Feeling the lick of firelight when The Master shared bread and fish with them,
Beneath heaven's wheeling lights, slathered with jewels of dew
In an open field when dawn's tapers made the eastern horizon blush pink and
gold,
Into the market stalls to buy food, past the inn's lintel to rent rooms?
When did these feet stop in mid-stride-literally or not-when the owner,
Who had heard the words, seen the miracles, listened to the sermons,
Seen the blind given sight, Lazarus throwing off the lineaments of death
Stiff-walking out of the tomb-when did sole/toe/ankle/instep
In the sojourner's heart-tamp the engine of belief's propulsion/movement
And the one carried by them say in his heart *I will go no further,*
I have gone far enough, and he is not what he was supposed to be,
He is not what I was given to believe that he would be,
Was it then that the morning/day/night's filth and dirt resisted
All basins, towels, soaps and oils-but remained moored in mud-slog,
The owner merely going froward in the most prosaic sense of the word,
Spirit stationary like a dying dune-anchored bloom amidst a creosote sea,

Fixed as the moon looking down on the tight mouth and open eyes
Lost in the ebb and tide of pride, the wheat-field whisper of resentment,
As tinder crackled, blanket snapped and the dreaming muttered.
I will go no further, I have gone far enough,
And he is not what he was supposed to be,
He is not what I was given to believe that he would be,
And I expected more deserved more we deserved more
Did Judas move his feet past the sheets' folds in a modest inn,
Toes striped by morning light, bruised and league-swollen, his mind,
Bereft of love, awe, teachings, parables, sermons, the defeat of Legion
(did he not go out with the others on the road no stick no beggar's bag)
And did he grind his teeth realizing that those feet would not stand next to
A radiant throat in the here and now, or stand on the red and yellow
Thunderbolt-marked mountain of the scutum shields of Roman dead,
That there would be no deference, no respect, no power power and power
On this side no mouth pressed to the royal ear no hand to hold the scepter,
Ambition reduced to shards like the nard of perfume the silly woman wasted.
Did he fish for the coin-bag that was always the hard proof of right-thinking:
How much they needed to spend, how much to hold back to keep them going,
The money was real-the money was necessary-and this is not what I thought
What I thought it would be-because money buys food, clothes, pays for inns,
For the blood of beasts, finances wars, buys swords, knives, spears, armor,
How long were we to waste time healing the sick and lame when we should take action,
Run Pilate and his crew back to Rome-lightning from the sky like Elijah against Ahaziah,
Melted eagle standards, blasted cuirass plates or blind like the Syrian army
When Elisha prayed that they be stricken blind-he can do it, we can do it,
This is not what I expected this is not what he was supposed to be
The kingdom the kingdom could be now now now
I will walk no further with him! I will not!
If the Lord had bathed Judas's feet along with The Twelve,
Would he have said to Himself, in pained tones:
These went with me, but you did not,
And neither hyssop or fuller's skill
Could ever make you clean.

MARTHA'S VINEYARD

They insisted they loved until love's need
Hit them like an orca's head slamming into
The prow of a kayak in open water
And then they said
No but take them away

KUMAGI NAOZANE

Who beheaded Prince Taira Atsumori at The Battle of Ichi-No-Tani During The
Gempei War And Repented And Became A Monk When He Found A Flute
On The Body of The Young Noble And Realized He Was The One in
The Taira Clan Ranks Who Had Played It Before The Battle
"There are tens of thousands of riders in our eastern armies, but I am sure none of
them has brought a flute to the battlefield. Those court nobles are refined men!"[3]

The Tale of Heike
The soul of Kumagi had joined the flute's song before the battle,
It had joined his blood's pulse before the horses tore down the cliff to the shore
host,
When the katanas sang their harsh rejoinder to the instrument's sweet refrain,
Like nightingale's flirtatious reply to moon shadow, like the castle wisteria to rain
skein,
Before the swords and lances flashed and quivered silver like a spackle of icefish
Beneath star-glittered waves, silver koi circling beneath pond's green and gold
mirror,
Death-poem in unrequited love to the horned, mustachioed helmet of the fated
poet.
The Minamoto samurai sat up in his stirrups squeezed between the windsock
wallop of banners,
Sun jouncing off his lacquered breastplate, the flute's notes filigreeing
The gaps in the air scribbled with the kanji of curses, boasts and pedigrees
declaimed,
Making his mouth go as big and wide as an *oni* mask as his hands tightened on
the reins

And he turned to the rough mountaineers around him, rubes riled up
To spill the blood of that insufferable clan of court aesthetes, the bitter foe that
oppressed them,
And when, moved as-spirit/head/heart pricked like the spur to his steed's flank,
The unlimbering s of a crane's neck amidst a rusty-voiced murder of crows and
jackdaws,
He made his awestricken comment-that in their ranks thick as summer green
bamboo,
There wasn't one samurai-one foot-soldier who would have blown the speech
Of a tender herald to their host now hooting and jeering like a bunch of monkey
tengu,
Bragging about the Taira heads they would tally for battle honors,
The death-wide eyes (skating ponds for flies!) they would pile at the feet of great
Yoritomo;
How they jittered impatiently in their saddles-their breastplates rubbing together,
Shrilling like cicadas, the spotted arrows on their backs rustling like buckwheat.
Transported by the flute's melancholy mizzle, did Kumagi rub a gauntleted hand
Against a black-blue beard point or a close shaved cheek and think to himself,
Who among us could make such music-could sit among the high-minded
Attending a Noh play and appreciate such things-feel the soul lift like a battle
plume
Of red over the moon crescent of a brave helmet and if we win today at Suma,
Where will the spirit that can coax music from a flute go when we have stained
The sands and breakers red with the blood of the refined and valiant Taira?
When will we hear such music after we chase the shattered stragglers to their
ships?
As he sat his horse on the cliff before the shore of Ichi-Noh-Tani,
Ears itching like a young hare's at the flute play's streams and eddies,
Did Kumagi consider the minutiae of life and focus his *hara*
On the ephemeral world that would fly like thistles in a few short moments?
What did his senses define before the hooves spat sand and descended to the
beach:
The deep orange of a tern's beak as the bird banked from the wink of their
weapons,
The startling red of a lychee's pebbly skin as a sun-bronzed foot-soldier
Pulled it out of his belt's scrip to demolish it with a few quick, sharp bites,

The deep blue watersheen of a dragonfly's body as it zig-zagged close by to hover before

The blue centipede mons blazoned on a warrior's yellow banner, winging away

On its spotted light-fired wings when a war-steed neighed impatiently in the next rank,

The breeze-sent spatter of sand granules in a helmet's bright braided orange beard,

The deep green of a fly on the trench of cheek scar of the lancer next to him,

The ethereal white of a stitched peonies pattern on a commander's purple sleeve;

Over the astringency of salt water, armor and sword oils and dried kelp, guano and fish rot,

Did he smell the thread-thin savor of beef soba drifting from out the enemy line,

The stink of horse manure and the overpowering miasma of human sweat,

The perfume of a dune-anchored wildflower, the tang of plum wine or tang of tea,

As someone hastily gulped it down, knowing it could be their last cup or flask?

As Kumagi watched the Taira bristling like the hedgehog behind their fortifications,

Could he hear, over the breakers-teased out by the flute's assay-the rasp

Of his fellow soldiers' respirations-like the groans of winter cedars in an ice-storm,

Layer after layer of *nembutsus* whispered through the frozen mouths of

Anthropomorphic helmet masks, the names of martial ancestors, the war gods

Hachiman (the Minamoto clan god) or Bishamon, did Kumagi, senses attuned,

Hear the silent intonement of a beloved's name beneath the battle patter,

Or those of a dear child, as he, Kumagi remembered his young son?

Later, when their charge broke the Taira ranks and rolled in fury across the beach,

After Kumagi called the retreating Prince Atsumori from the shame of the breakers,

Made him disdain the surf's sough, the fleeing ships with wind-billowed sails

(how many swallowtail butterflies on mast canvas took flight that cruel day!),

The Minamoto samurai beckoning with his black battle fan painted with a gold rondel,

And Atsumori wheeled his steed to meet Kumagi in a blizzard of steel and sinew.

How did the fight go between those notables-drawn out or brief and vicious?

How did the dance go on that bloody shingle, curlews and sandpipers running

Back and forth like war pages with fresh weapons and mounts, as all around them,
The rest of the battle raged: the bravest of the opposing samurais shouting out
Their lineage and superiority (along with the usual base and wearisome insults)
Did anyone stop to watch as the Minamoto man bested and disarmed his Taira foe,
Shucked off his helmet as a gull shells a lobster of its head and carapace?
Did anyone recognize a particularly fluid move as emblematic of a particular teacher,
Suck their breath in at a close call, a fast duck, or shout "finish it up-we're not done, yet!"
Only the two martial hearts that met that day can answer-and they are both dust!
Kumagi, seeing he had a young prince in hand, a hawk chick out of the egg,
Whose chiseled features, eyes dark as pools of whale oil, long hair shiny as black pine
After an evening rain, face powdered, teeth blackened in the imperial way,
Reminded him of his son, around the same age as the Taira royal,
And due to this, and the youth's high spirits that made him boast that anyone
Among the chief Minamoto officers would recognize his head and assign Kumagi
The best of war honors, that samurai, moved in his soul, stayed his blade.
Like a sword cord in the sea-breeze, Atsumori's fortunes swung this way and that.
Had the flute's song bestirred compassion and appreciation of life in Kumagi's breast,
Reminded him of the absurdity of a world where beauty and bloodshed shared stage
As a dowager courtesan and her understudy the same irascible client's needs,
The flycatcher singing in a font of lavender about to be pulled down by a badger's dig?
How ridiculous and wonderful was existence-how absurd and sad!
How quick and fleeting everything beautiful or ugly made under heaven:
Spring cherry blossoms, concentric circles fanning out from a frog pond,
Even the warm and incomparable impress of a first kiss-nothing lasts!
Poor Kumagi! How could he save the Taira prince when his own comrades,
Rushing forward like torrents after a spring thaw or gulls for a basket of fresh smelt,
Clamored for the choice trophy, swords quivering in their hands like the fan

Of a court beauty who is receiving chrysanthemums and plaudits from a lover,
And shakes in modesty and ardor on a castle stair, so did the weapons
Of these victorious mountain hicks tremble-each man pushing his fellow aside
To take the prize-what could Kumagi do but content himself with the knowledge
That he would pray for Atsumori for the rest of his life, so he raised his blade
And in a glittering arc sent the prince's soul sailing away like the swallowtail
mons of his house,
Ah, it was a bitter flight for the butterfly that had just emerged from its chrysalis
And flexed its gorgeous black and yellow wings before the valiant of the day!
And as his body fell, his flute slipped from the folds of his arming-coat,
Cushioned by the blood-speckled grains and mussel and clam shell slivers.
Kumagi's heart was cut to the quick when he looked down and saw the length
Of polished bamboo lying by the young noble, and realized that it was he
Who had played with such skill and emotion, weaving through the waiting ranks,
Deep calling to deep-who would have thought this should be? How cruel was
Life!
Such a small thing this duel and what a great thing it was in the korm of human
change!
Was there one Minamoto trooper here who could have coaxed such perfection,
Struck the finger-holes with their calloused, grubby fingers and with dexterity,
Sent such well-knelled warblers among the eagles bracing each other beak to
beak!
Who among these mountaineers fated to take the day and end this clan,
Could have played a charming riposte to send the cultured ones slinking?
In truth, the flute of Atsumori accomplished far more than what his sword could,
When those wind-wafted notes carried in their pure and liquid form to Kumagi,
They killed ego and world-things-promotion, head tallies, glories of bravery
scrolls,
The first breath on the first hole-first suspiration had assured Kuamgi's surrender:
The orange monk's robes, shaven poll and the mala beads that would end the
warrior,
The negation of the Martial Man Who Was, for the Man of Repentance and
Spirit,
Who wept when he delivered the swift sentence to his enemy and in the moment
of truth,

Threw his sword away like a disgusted fisherman tossing a basket of scrawny sea-
bream
Back into the waves, or a stooped and elderly gardener heaving a rotten winter
melon
Onto a manure heap-that was what how Kumagi reckoned his life,
When Atsumori's head fell like a sunflower, death's stroke upholding the proof of
his art:
There was the "Saeda" ("The little Branch) among the slain prince's belongings:
The flute that was passed down by Emperor Toba to Taira no Tadamori.
It was like a loosed arrow striking another, changing the trajectories of both
whittled darts,
Two Hinoki cypresses storm-slammed into one another, uprooted and flung
together.
Two souls knocked askance by the sad meeting of sword and song.
Ha! What chance did the razor-edged blade of the Minamoto have:
The blade fittings-habaki/seppa/tsuba-not undone (the sword undone)
The blade's wrapped hilt pattern (the tsuka ito) unraveled for good in its owner's
hand,
Before a single blow was struck-before the commanders' fans swept down in
decision.
The sword was traded for the flute then-the breastplate and helm for the orange
priest's robes,
The recognition of shared humanity had been entwined in that masterful coda
Produced by the slim fingertips and breath of the courtier who shared his soul on
Suma beach.
Kumagi, soon disillusioned with the Minamoto leader Yoritomo, would shave his
queue,
Take up the calling of monk, saying nembutsus for all those whom he had slain,
And all of his days, he would be a deft player of the saeda.

INSPIRATION

Sometimes inspiration comes quickly
Imagine the dynamism of a piece of Frank Frazetta art
A cowpoke on paint horse on a winding mountain trail
The horse rearing up in equine shock and fear mane flying front hooves lashing
out
Broiling robin blue and the odd scudding puff of cumulus overhead
And the cowboy is spinning in the saddle Colt revolvers blazing away
Barrels spitting orange-red fire sunlight helixing off the saddle horn as he empties
them
Into the tawny cougar flying out of a screen of green sage and chola front claws
splayed
Fangs gleaming pink mouth open in a snarl of animal rage black pupils catching
glints
In slit braise of shining teal eyes dust trailing from the back claws
Cat's dun face scribbled with white ears tipped with day-glare
To the left of the trail nothing but a sheer drop to rock and river
Some upthrust fangs of stone riddled with chapparal in the distance
Cat and cowboy/dinner or a pelt for the trading-post down the mountain.
Now and then it's that easy and you lower the hammer on the cat
The marriage and meld of meter and mellifluence hitting the bullseye
Or maybe it's a struggle like the cowboy and puma locked in combat
Gone over the edge in a brief billow of dust and grit flashing conchos and claws
Freefall to the snake-wind of green sun-scalloped river rush broken by stone
Cowboy's free hand pushing the fang-split maw away while the other
Has whipped out a big buck from the belt scabbard and is
Looking for a soft spot in the cat's deep red-brown chest

While one of the cougar's front paws has stitched a line of red fire
Across the man's leather vest and the other hooked into a shoulder
While the back ones row the air as the man's hair flies upwards
His mouth drawn in a furious rictus hate-filled eyes matching the cat's green gaze
As water and stone comes up to meet them and maybe if we're looking down
We could have a couple of surprised rock ravens scattering on the wind
Squawking and shedding black feathers as the two plummet past spurs winking silver
A patch of blood on the cougar's flank from a bullet's graze tossing up tiny red swirls
I could definitely see that sometimes the mind has to fight hard to make the art
The swivel in the saddle and quick blow-out giving way to grapple and gravity.
And then there are days when what comes is the horse with its askew saddle
Dissapearing around the corner of the trail, hooves sending up thin plumes of dust
The Colts lying on the trail sprinkled by drizzles of blood that become a swath
An uneven trail of scarlet freshets and reddish dirt beads as we watch the cougar
Teeth sunk into the shoulder of the cowboy sprawled face down
Dragging the man's body up the incline of sage and chola to its (unseen) den
Its back legs braced the sun bringing out bits of foundry fire from back fur
And muzzle the black ear tips black to the point of looking blue
Maybe there's a trout scale of shine on a polished leather boot
A crushed black hat lying close to an outflung hand its silver band badly scuffed
And already moving in looking for their piece of the pie
A couple of vultures lighting down jaundiced yellow beaks split
Greasy wings fanning dust drift pink wattles etched in blue and black
As the cougar strains showing the flow and tense of feline musculature
While its dragging its prey up and away from the trail
Looking up at us like the uptilted eyes as on a Chinese mask
Maybe we will add some mystery here and leave a silver locket
In the foreground where the buzzards are about to touch down
And we will be left wondering whose picture is inside.
(maybe the cowboy and cougar were never the inspiration)
(maybe it was the locket all along a mystery left unplumbed)
You have those days when you are sitting inside the house on
A breathtaking autumn day of sharp light cold wind and leaf whirl

And you know in your bones you won't blast the cat with one fluid move
That you are going to go from monitor to kitchen refilling the coffee mug
Either you go over the side cold water and mica-flecked canyon waiting for you
Or you get hauled into the den wit and word-weft gone for now
Nothing but the hook of a claw pad in your back and shafts of dirty light
Breaking on the lip of the entry ledge.

RAPTURE

Stop trying to predict when it's going to happen:
You don't know, I don't know, no one knows the date and the time,
When it's going down-day, night, dawn, twilight, hour of the wolf
Or second of the Lamb-it doesn't do to mark off the calendar, folks.
When you are plucked up with the others, purloined and para-sailed
Out of everything you know/out of this world/out of the regard
Of those who love you, hate you, are indifferent to you-Gone is Gone,
There will be no warning, no message limned in midnight's Northern Light,
When you're airlifted out of the diesel dreams of human revels, ecstasies and
griefs,
It ends when you're grabbed, lofted into light and love by the empyrean hand of
God,
Joining the convocation of souls, air-marching/moving in cloud cadence.
How can we describe what it means to meet the Lord in the air?
How can you describe with mortal words and mindset
The joy of The Church raptured/taken from above/translated,
The old life/flesh/bone/cells atomized/gusted into granules,
Medevac'd/Ezekiel-wheeled into the waiting arms of The Son?
We cannot imagine the transmogrification of our current existence
When we are overwhelmed by heaven's indescribable ambuscade,
Hammered into spirit's new skin of pure alchemized gold,
The falling away of the last dry twists of this earth's umbilical cords,
Experience's cracked walnut scent replaced by Home's evening primrose,
Summer honeysuckle-the old no more, the old us no more.
In the meantime, share The Good News and just be prepared
To be prepared to never be prepared-no one's going to know when
They step out of the play and the director tells the set man to unhook the stars.

REPENTANCE

Romans 6:18
English Standard Version
[18] and, having been set free from sin, have become slaves of righteousness.
"The past is never dead. It isn't even past."
William Faulkner

Our sorrow and grief over Old Sin remains, annealed
Like the scarlet caste mark of a New Delhi street-vendor:
It doesn't go away-it resurfaces with varying regularity,
When we behold the natural face in the glass of regard.
Even when we have experienced the incomprehensible grace of God,
The Son's gift, bestowed through the blood and the dogwood cross,
We recall from time to time the ignominy of The Old Heart,
Sitting like a desiccated still-life-a rotten lemon on a sideboard,
Spotted with mini archipelagoes of greenish gray mold,
Next to a burnished samovar and a slice of mother-of-pearl nautilus.
We remember when we were (in enmity),
We remember the things we did (in enmity).
Like a millionaire who has gone on to a pristine palazzo,
But can't help touring the mean streets of his old haunts now and then,
To find that the family home has become a crack den.
Memories of youth's evils and selfishness return
Like the snapshots of some resplendent, moon-silvered whirl
Of white-pink cherry blossoms scattered across a stream or
The palimpsest of a poisoner's art hiding under a fresh love poem,

Waking from night sweats to itch a phantom limb.
But we need to be careful so we do not insult The Son:
Too much reflection on The Old Man can be an affront to God,
And weariness to the spirit that should be rejoicing
Over the maul that broke the shackles and freed you from eternal censure.
There's a narcissism: like standing on the back porch after night's rain,
To enjoy the moon's halo and the tentative strains of a warbler's song,
Only to start at the ragged yips and snarls of a coyote pack chorus
Drifting in with the from the park beyond the block.
Regrets bore into us like the cancerous seed of a shoulder mole:
Remembering when we shooed away the better angels our nature like
The gnats and midges in twilight's gloam.
We remember when we could have loved and lived better,
As if we could go back to those windy, briar-blown crossroads,
And taken a queue from some inward-powered GPS to take a new turn,
Spy an indigent with prophet's beard and tattered coat holding a sign,
The warning light-spackle of a trooper's top bubble-the chatter of grackle
From a roadside screen of winter-blasted mulberry trees,
As if we could go back, and make the good save and heal the ones we hurt,
Find an honest open door-the aperture of poultice/balm/surgery
To gather up each one and take them to their healing pool of Siloam,
Sped across a long field, arms outstretched to catch a young woman
Flung from out a plane's explosion-her hair a medusa's cap of streaming locks,
And lower her to a bed of yellow lilies or yarrow-the right words of comfort
On our lips-the words honed by hoisting hearts out of storm-lashes messes
Of broken spars and masts-yes, there are times we recall the old sins of The Old
Heart,
Because repentance makes ambulance drivers (with past dispatchers) of us all,
It makes hospital buskers of us all-spending songs in the burn wards
Of our sorrows, the intensive care units of our being.
God says: withstand yourself and sin no more.
I paid for it all: the shame included.
There is an end to watching bad drive-in features
On a landfill's lip.
There is an end to touring midnight zoos.
But there arc times

We remember when we spat

On a proffered love pure as a Pegasus touching down to earth,

And we say to ourselves *had I been then as I am now*

Had I been then thank you God I am not now as I was then

I am not now as I was then

I am

Not now

TAKING MARK FOR A WALK IN THE PARK

When you give everyone a voice and give people power, the system usually ends
up in a really good place. So, what we view our role as, is giving people that power.
Mark Zuckerberg

Sometimes, I wish I could take Mr. Zuckerberg for a morning walk
Not in the chainmail-gray days of autumn but in brindled spring or summer,
Around our local Mile Square or maybe Huntington Beach Central Park,
Point out the finches trilling away in the elms, bellies the brash blood hue
Of the palm-framed horizon bands of a Miami sunset,
Sweep a hand (with less generosity but as much respect)
At the gaggles of black-headed Canadian geese, honking querulously
Like drivers trapped in grill-to-grill Los Angeles rush-hour traffic
As they bully the charcoal-colored ibis' out a lush grass patch.
I would point out the coots croaking somnolently at the lake's edge,
The mallards and their dames quaking away in a reed-curtained mud pond,
Or tug Mr. Zuckerberg's sleeve to register the breeze-tossed skirls,
Of red-tailed hawks gaging death's dividends, speckled undersides shining,
Fringed wings touched with sun-fire as they go about their fateful spirals.
Of course, you can't fairly compare hawk-song to a sparrow circle:
That is like trying to match the fateful boom of a *Noh*-play drum to the
Wild abandon and reverie of a string symphony or a piano concerto,
But they both have a *right* to be heard, yes? (raptor or yapper)
Everyone in The World of Bird gets their Word in, first or last.
Later, circumnavigating the joggers, bicyclists and dog-walkers,
I would stab a finger upwards at the scads of black phoebes and bluebirds

In the vernal awnings of the sugar gum and eucalyptus,
Cheeping and whistling with the desperate joy of troubadours
For a bowl of greasy mutton and leek soup bestowed by a stingy feudal lord,
And at that point with a weariness-yes, a weariness I can hardly describe,
It is then I would turn to Mr. Zuckerberg with respect and say,
Listen to the spirit-lifting lilts, modulations, cadencies of the avian world,
The variety, the beauty, the improvisation, the utter transcendence
Of each free program offered every day and eve, without the tender
Of a single copper-their payment just our appreciation for their part
In this amazing world of light and love. So, I would say:

God has given them a voice, Mr. Zuckerberg.
Why can't we have ours?

CHILDHOOD MEMORY

I remember gasping for air on my back
Sprawled on my grandparents' bed
And my grandmother holding my salvation aloft
Like Thetis raising little Achilles' heel
Before plunging him into the river Styx
Blue as the Lapus Lazuli of
Egyptian judges and kings
Vicks VapoRub

CHILDHOOD MEMORY/CARPENTER BEE

I can recall to this day sitting in the infant's highchair
At the dinner table in the cramped Compton house's kitchen
And the fire-drill drum of feet and panic-the frenzied back and forth
Of agitated bodies silverfish wink of yellow, jaundiced light
The deliquescence of humidity/night turning the screen door
Into a slab of darkness and yes, I sat there watching it all helplessly
As hands bearing dish towels and napkins went up to
Smack/intercept/down/catch the back bullet form of
The carpenter bee that had entered the kitchen
As it zinged from one corner of the kitchen to the other
Wound up ricocheting and doing whirlies like the last contested grape
Jouncing across the fingertips of Roman patricians
Vying for possession of it in a villa's marble hall.
There was the bee searching for an exit,
There was me, stuck in the highchair,
Watching in awe, not a swatter, towel or Gerber's bottle at hand,
Incapable of contributing my nascent mettle to the bee-hunt.
I remember this as vividly as I recall the face of
Kimberly J. from the 6th grade: she of the moth-soft eyes,
High forehead, tumbling waterfall of brown tresses, tumescent lower lip
Whom I believed that God in heaven had used as the physical template
For the angelic host. If perfection existed on earth, *then she was it.*
I am an old man and have forgotten many things,
But I will remember the carpenter bee and Kimberly J.
To the day I die. The bee and the girl remain conjoined
In my memory whether they would have wanted to be or not,

My elderly mind mounding a redoubt about them both
As axons, neurons and synapses go about the long and untidy
Work of long-term brain-death. I just *remember*.
And the end came when it did not with a bang or a whimper
But the anticlimax of surrender and self-negation.
The end came and when it did it the bee opted out
Embracing his (or her) intrinsic bee-honor like the pilot
Of a Japanese Mitsubishi A6M2 Zero deciding to plunge
Into the blue scintillant net of the vast Pacific's swells
Rather than go back to his carrier with his jammed guns
And no ship or plane tally to show for his efforts in the dogfight.
Eluding the last hand swipes and whip-snap of cloth
It executed a loop the loop with aplomb and grace
Beneath the ceiling lights over the table before
Landing smack in the middle of the big bowl
Of potato salad sitting amidst the clutter of dishes and plates
To the groans and howls of disgust of those who had
Been cheated of laying down some serious insect whoop-ass.
There was the dead or dying bee, black and shiny as an olive
Mired in the bee-killing mustard morass of potato salad,
About to be fished out and slung out into the squamous night,
Leaving nothing to his name but an empty burrow in the dirt.
And there was me, stuck in my highchair, a mere infant,
Momentarily forgotten in the pantomime of adult shape and bug whirr,
Unable to grasp the tragic, striking dichotomy between
The relative ease of ingress and the distress of egress,
The seconds between evasive grace and fatal pratfall.
I could not see the comedy of it all, the absurdity,
I could not even feel sorry for the bee.
I simply *was*-unlike the bee-and all I could calculate
Was the mysterious relationship of time/space/motion
Between food, spoons, bibs and trays.
Maybe it is an autumn thought and this
In its own way is an autumn poem:
I see very few carpenter bees these days.
There are times it makes me sad.
One day I will remember neither the bee or the girl.

ARGONAUT AT REST

When he was an old man, the Greek hero Jason sought out the remains of the Argo,
The vessel that bore him and the argonauts to great glory and triumph. Jason was killed
when the ship's stern fell on him as he brooded amidst the wreckage.

I have been thinking of late of the Greek hero Jason, son of Aeson,
In his last days when he sought the sleep-shade of his former fame,
The sea/salt-nibbled stern of the Argo, that great ship of his high missions,
Now brought to naught but the sad frame-whittled hold that once held heroes.
I can see him stumbling through the shallows of that shingle,
The spill of lush star-fields on high tide's hurly drawing him on,
He who led the argonauts to adventure and the quest for the Golden Fleece,
The one-sandaled man prophesized to unseat his father's killer, King Pelias,
King of Thessaly-sworn to the gilt goat's recoup/the winged ram's skin, coat-hung
In Colchis, bivouacked ebullition of Aeetes shining in the dragon's glade,
The great achievement crowning those set for him by Pelias and Colchis' ruler.
How could it be that the son of Aeson who assayed such deeds,
Come to this, picking through the sand and shell bits like a wind-ruffled godwit
For the tidbits of high-tide's tumble-how could it come to this?
How sad, I thought, when heroes go bad and hang on to the shadow of a name
Turned tawdry through base intent and wedding-oath's wounding;
The great wound of soiled reputation that stayed on him like a pilotfish on a
shark,
Brought him back to the font of achievement, shaken by years' scythe
To thin timbers on the shore's mont-as if coming back to the Argo
Like a repentant husband could heal his tremoring heart of its hurts,
That the old boat would be buoyed by the old magic of wave, romance,

Sun, surf, kinship of company, new labors and new sands.

Now down and out after his treachery to Medea had turned her to filicide.

Here, the hero muttering like a transient gone to tipple of cheap rye,

Made his way through the sand and seaweed heaps to make a pillow's mound

Beneath the star-kissed stern of Argus' hard work, Dodona's sacred oak

Merely a whisp of the god-wood the Argive joined to the prow through

Athena's aegis-nothing now but wind-blasted spar/hold/canvas strips.

The speaking wood from Zeus' grove had nothing to impart to the old hero,

The shavings of sure advice and sagacity that had served Jason well time afore,

Were no more than the high keen of kestrel and gull, the song of the sea's lyre.

The oars made from Mount Pelion's pines had fed beach fires long ago,

Girded with dry seaweed to make light cairns for night's convoys.

Where were Nereus' daughters with their sweet song to cheer the man

In the begrimed chiton coming back to earth's bulwarks to mourn

The ship-grave where youth, valor, hard muscle and heaven's fortune

Had provided breath's bait and sweet billows for the sail canvas-to do great
things,

To procure justice against proud Pelias who unjustly held his throne?

Here was a man weighed down by sorrows careering to dementia's drop,

Lurching after the time and sea-leeched leavings of old bravura's ghost,

Right mission's closure moldering in the elements' cruel clasp,

But he went forward, to reckon youth's victories and betrayal's toll.

Surely, he wandered in moonlight, hating Helios' horses-the advent of light,

The solar deity was the grandfather of Medea the child-slayer,

And had borne her away from her husband's vengeful wrath,

So, what could dawn's morning ramble of cloud-rift and beam but remind him

Of the child-light scrubbed from his days, made away by the mother

As noon's pellucid pass on still water is overthrown by storm's show?

How could the captain of that crew of heroes, who joshed with Hercules,

Meleager and Peleus in the gunnels, stand the memory of the prow's knife

Spraying morning's sea-beads gold as amber across the deck hands,

Sun-dogs making a long salver of the sea's mirror, as the fickle dolphins

Raced alongside the smart vessel, weaving through the wave-weft?

How could Jason, remembering the sky-clout of Helios' steeds

And the escape of the filicide not come to loath the daystar's fiery drive?

How could he not come crawling to the Argo by moonlight, a heliophobe

Now given to night-wander-weak moon-balm his heart of palm in old age.
And how could Jason-a hero gone wrong-stand the crimson enfilade
Of sunset: did he not see the blood of his dear ones in the arterial lacquer
Winding around the boughs of pine, olive and oak with the sun's russet assay?
How could the winner of the fleece-gilt, the one who dared the clashing rocks
That killed unwary mariners, the slayer of harpies who moved Orpheus to lyre's
fire,
Not crave a hoodie or serge cowl's shadow during the early/ending hours?
I hold that he rested his head, no more capped by bronze and ostrich plumes,
But belling with anguish and misery like a sea-cave's ribs with tide treble,
He rested it on a soothing patch of moon-solder amidst the broken hold's canvas
heap,
Under the curved stern's tail that waited for him like deferred doom,
Like a loyal dog gone wrong and feral waiting to go for an old master's throat.
Heart-sore with the remembrance of past infidelities accrued like pledges,
His hopes in Corinth dashed with the burnt bride-bones in the death-dress
Given as a gift by the cast-aside daughter of Aeetes-how could he not groan
At the jounce of morning's chariot-trail of gold and rose in the east heights?
Nothing had healed him of horrors that motored placidly though his brain
Like the weedy seadragons among the mess of mysid shrimp and plankton.
He returned to the source of yearning-when he, the youth shorn of one shoon,
Watched with joy as heroes homed to him at the mast spread,
Eager to aid him against the usurper-so here he was, an old man,
Weather-beaten by prodigies pulled on strange shores, used up,
No hope to cast-off-his life a dead wake, a weak wave's slap on the hull's skin,
Could a better casket/cairn/catafalque be found than the Argo's grit-piled guts.
None walked the aft deck but the tern, the gull and the cormorant:
These were sad companions for the son of Aeson who had shipped out
With champions and demi-gods, high-minded conscripts made for renown.
I think Jason was relieved when the timeworn stern gave way
As he sat, skull mounded with ragged cloak and cold sand,
Looking up at the icy and indifferent patterns of the constellations,
The sob and drum of night surf in his ears-the wind-shift of dunes
Doubling down with the chill gusts coming off the combers.
Did he ask-as has been said-that the cloud-convoller Zeus to end his pain?
Olympus' king knew the convolutions of broken wedding bonds

As much as the great hero did, and had no such repair for himself,
The adulterer comfy with swan down, satyr-skin or pismire's armor,
Always trying to stay one step ahead of Hera's ire and suspicion,
Leaving a wake of wounded and transmogrified one-night stands.
Would he have had pity on the old hero who had wanted a shoe,
And had won so much, only to lose all in the dismayed upgrade
Of wife and life because Corinth offered a social-climber's delight
In the chance to be part of the royal line-well, I don't think so:
I don't think Zeus would have had mercy on a fellow philanderer,
Would have given a blue finger-bolt or bid Aeolis to blow down
The ship's tail to put the gray adventurer out of his misery.
The selfish don't throw a crumb dribble to the pigeons or old hound,
So I rather think Zeus didn't give a thought to Jason's pity-fest,
Not when the hearth-queen had made it clear she would never forgive him
For casting aside Aeetes' daughter after she had given all that he might bear
The gold-wooled coverlet of green-skiened Poseidon's pride.
No, I think it was just the marriage of Time and Terrible Timing,
That brought the Argo's stern down-ship timber and mind's timber's meet,
The fateful greet of wind-whittled kindling and the almond-shaped amygdala.
It wasn't some divinely devised full-circle folly that he was fated to suffer,
Any more than there was meaning implicit in the writ of water and sand,
The pirouette and twist of winkle and cockle shells in night tide's ebb.
The master of the Argo had simply picked a bad night to go on a bender,
To think a morbid wallow in the old hull would be less lacerating
Than the march of mundane days that reminded him of what he had been.
Once the stern shattered his skull to potsherd shards-brickle of bone and gore,
Neither the sand lice or the crabs or night birds forebore to move in,
The victor over the six-armed Geigenes, tamer of the fire-breathed Khalkotauroi
Meant no more to them than that of a seal carcass or pelican,
None heard the ghostly pass of Hercules' club, the light, liquid slap of
Water-walking Euphemus' feet or the call of cattle-breaking Augeas.
There was no shroud of honor, resplendent as the armor of Meleager
To spare the great captain from the predations of those who give worms work.
The ship's bit offered no judgment-it just came down without ceremony,
Without rancor, without love, without pity, as a tern's beak
On the carapace of a lobster-over was over in the hull's trash

While the moon passed on its way-as neuter as the constellations.
None said *is this the man who paid Pelias the winged ram's wool,*
The promised throne-coin for Thessaly's solemnities?
But I wonder if just as the stern did its fatal work,
If there was a moment-swift as the afterimage of lightning tines on the retina,
When a single memory returned: before the betrayal of bed and bond,
The cold shoulder, cold eye and epithets "alien," and "barbarian,"
Applied to the beloved, applied to the one who had given all,
So he could be free to court Creusa, fragrant as the Bear's Breech,
If
It
Didn't
Come
Back
To him
Before
Starlight
Wood fall
Pate's break
Happiness as sun-butter bright as the golden oriole's breast,
The ram's skin flaring from the mast's hide semaphoring magma's braise,
Fellow heroes tanned black as charred pine hedging him in at the prow,
And there he was, leaning forward, smiling with affection,
His quest-calloused hand stretched out, to brush the fingertips
Of the young woman with wind-tousled locks of jet waiting to board,
Her chiseled features limned with adoration and hope, Hecate's witch-fire
Playing around the rims of her olive-dark iris, lips moist as Cyclades grapes,
Curve of columnar neck bearing the marks of her prince's kisses,
Small bottles of tinctures, draughts and potions clinking in her side-bag,
Gathered up before she could suffer the fall of the tidal wrath of Aeetes,
I wonder if Jason remembered saying these words:
"I will replace the home you lose this day."
"The Argives will love you as I do. No one will call you exile or barbarian."
"I will never leave you as long as Pyrois, Aeos, Aethon and Phlegon
Draw your grandfather's chariot across the sky.
I give you my word from this day on."

THE LEGACY MEDIA

Me: Give me all the truth that I can bear.
The Legacy Media: No, but cast us out, that we may go into the swine.